Cougars at the Beach

A Mickke D Grand Strand Murder Mystery

A work of fiction

Steve McMillen

This book is a work of fiction. Names, characters, places and incidents are either products of the author's imagination or are used fictitiously and are not to be construed as real. Any resemblance to actual events, locales or persons, living or dead, is entirely coincidental.

ISBN: 1499320329
ISBN 13: 9781499320329
Library of Congress Control Number: 2014910442
CreateSpace Independent Publishing Platform
North Charleston, South Carolina

"It's always fun to read about places you know so everyone who lives in the Myrtle Beach area or who has vacationed here, should love *Cougars at the Beach* by Steve McMillen. From Little River to Pawleys Island, and even the Myrtle Beach Boardwalk, it's all here. Combine it all with a little romance and a serial killer and you have yourself a great beach read. You may be so absorbed your feet may never hit the water."

Diane DeVaughn Stokes, Television and Radio Host and Producer

"Steve McMillen's second book *Cougars at the Beach* is the perfect, easy to read, fun, vacation beach read. The murder mystery includes quite a bit of local history and local features, which anyone who lives here or has ever visited the beach will recognize."

Jody MacKenzie, Publisher/Editor Grand Strand Magazine

"A fast-paced follow-up to McMillen's premiere book, *Cougars at the Beach* is a sexy and satisfying thriller."

T. Lynn Ocean, author of novels including *Southern Poison* and *Southern Peril.*

Dedication

This book is dedicated again to my lovely bride Beverly. I also want to thank my editor and I want to thank everyone in my writer's group for the past five plus years. They kept me focused and got me through several writing trials and tribulations.

PROLOGUE

Early evening is making its appearance in the jungle outside of Bogota, Colombia. Drug cartel kingpin Senior Pablo Valdez calls to order a meeting of ten of his most trusted allies. They have come to his villa by personal invitation. The two-story, 8,000-square-foot mansion sits on 300 acres among heavy jungle vegetation and is located nearly one mile off the main road. It has a soccer field, riding stables, a large pool area, and helicopter pad. A gated and guarded entrance is part of an eight-foot-high concrete wall around the cleared five acres where the estate is located. The entire front entrance of the wall has cameras facing out toward the only road leading into the villa. Unless you happen to be flying over, there is no way of knowing the estate is there. The entire perimeter of the estate is posted with large private property, no trespassing signs. Several guards patrol the perimeter of the 300 acres on 4X4s 24 hours a day. One-half mile back, the only road in is a fortified guarded gate. The guards stationed there have automatic weapons and full communication with the villa. Unbeknownst and not noticeable to most visitors, there is a back way in and out, which only the inhabitants know about. The route is a pedestrian trail through the jungle to a narrow dirt road one-half mile away. The road leads to a paved landing strip long enough for Senior Valdez's Learjet.

Senior Valdez holds up his hand and asks for quiet between puffs on his Cuban cigar. The room immediately becomes still and attentive. "I have asked you to come here this evening because I still have a problem. The man who burned my cocaine and killed fourteen of my people several years ago is still alive. I recently received word that the man I sent to the United States to kill my enemy is dead. I just want all of you to know that the $250,000 reward is still in effect. I don't care if you kill him or you have someone else kill him as long as my name is not mentioned. All I want is proof that he is dead. A newspaper article will be more than adequate. As you leave, I have provided a file on him with his picture, description, name, and address in the U.S. If you decide to go, I will pay for your transportation to the U.S. and provide you with a passport. However, if you fail, if you do not provide proof of his death directly to me, do not return to Colombia. Thank you for coming." There is a low murmur as the ten invited guests exit the room, pick up their files, and leave the estate.

Miguel Sanchez opens his file and reads the first page:

Wanted - Dead not Alive, Mickke MacCandlish, aka Mickke D, Little River, South Carolina, age mid-forties, former Green Beret, 6' 1", 185 pounds with sandy brown hair. You should consider him armed and dangerous. He killed the last man we sent to the U.S. to eliminate him, a former Colombian soldier who worked under First Lieutenant MacCandlish while he was stationed in Colombia posing as a training consultant with the Colombian Army. His real job was to try to stop cocaine shipments to the U.S. We put the bounty on his head and tried several times to eliminate him while he was in Colombia, but all efforts failed. Page 2 is an 8 x 10 military photo of the intended target.

Miguel rubs his hands together, grins, and thinks it is about time for him to take a vacation. Since Senior Valdez is willing to buy him a ticket and provide a passport, why not go to the U.S.? He will kill this gringo and live the life of luxury in Colombia with the reward.

Chapter 1: The Hunter

The sun propels its first shafts of sunlight, brightening the sky from violet, to salmon, to blue as early morning dawns in the mountains of Colorado. A deafening silence claims the cold, thin, clean air.

A female cougar is stalking a snowshoe rabbit. She has been on the rabbit's trail since the sky turned from dark to pale. She finally spots her prey about 100 yards away. She has been using her keen sense of smell up to this point and now finally she has her first meal in three days in sight. All of her senses go viral. Her taunt muscular body is ready to pounce, her pupils are wide open, and her ears are at attention. She flexes her razor sharp claws in the freshly fallen snow.

However, she doesn't want to rush to the kill. She needs to get closer before she lunges for the final assault. The cougar moves with quiet stealth to get nearer to her prey. She gets to within fifty yards of the rabbit when he turns and sees her crouching in the snow. He cowers with fear and anticipation. She freezes; the wind is motionless and there is not a hair moving on her beautiful coat of winter fur.

The rabbit is upwind so he cannot smell the cougar but he senses danger. Should he run or maybe what he sees is just a boulder lying in the snow. The cougar can wait no longer; however, just as she is about to launch her attack a shot rings out and echoes through the narrow valley. The cougar does not move. She is dead, a shot through the heart. She should have been more concerned about being the prey rather than hunting her prey. The hunter has become the hunted.

The rabbit's ears go up at the sound of the rifle being fired, but he does not move. Fear overrides his sense of self-preservation. Another shot rings out and the rabbit collapses in the freshly fallen snow. Two pools of crimson red mar the pristine white snow covered landscape.

The human hunter grins. This is just sport to him, just a game. He will let both animals lie in the snow to become food for other predators. He packs up his rifle and proceeds back to his warm log cabin in the deep Colorado woods.

Once the hunter returns home, he sits down and enjoys a nice hot cup of coffee. He set the timer on the coffee maker before he left to coincide with his anticipated return. As he sips his hot coffee, he decides it is time to make some major decisions. He needs a change of scenery; it is time for him to move on with his life, which has become stale and rusty.

The hunter lives on sixty acres of mostly wooded land twenty miles away from the nearest town. He is divorced from his wife of ten years and has been living alone for the last five years, after she got "cabin fever" living out in the woods with no one to talk to but her husband. Actually, he never really wanted to talk much, just have sex.

That was fun for a while but she yearned for a more social type of life. She wanted friends, to go out to dinner occasionally, and maybe take in a movie. Also, her husband became more and more demanding. Over time she became overwhelmed by his need for sex. He turned into a person she did not enjoy being around and she became fearful of him so she gave him a choice: They move closer to town or she moves alone. He elected to stay so she left, but before she left, he told her she would regret her decision someday.

Now all he does is hunt in the winter and fish in the summer. He has his retirement from his former career in the government and a $500.00-a-month lease payment from a cell phone company. They had approached him about locating a tower on his land to complete a grid and he agreed after asking for one concession. He wanted them to install a wireless satellite repeater on the top of the tower so he could get on the internet with his computer. He used it to keep up with what's going on in the world and watch porn. Since his wife left, he has had very little female companionship. His occasional flings are usually just one-night stands; the women never seem to come back for a second date.

As the years pass, he gets bored hunting animals, catching fish, and watching porn. He feels the urge to pursue bigger prey, women. He can hunt them, use them, and hurt them without killing them. However, part of him thinks that might be interesting also.

He uses Google to find out where there is a large number of widows and available women in the U.S., in a warm climate. One of his searches brings up Myrtle Beach, South Carolina. The other locations were in or near large metropolitan areas. Myrtle Beach wins the lottery.

He decides to cut all ties with his Colorado home. He sells the land, house, and all of the furnishings, but retains the monthly lease money from the cell phone company.

Before leaving Colorado, he needs to do a couple of things. The first thing is to make changes in his appearance and take dancing lessons. He realizes the young and mature, rich, single, divorced, or widowed women like to dance and have sex, though not necessarily in that order. If any of them treat him like his ex-wife did, he will kill them and allow them to rot, just like the cougar and the rabbit.

He is a very resourceful man with some very refined skills, so his second chore is to venture into town and cut his wife's brake lines just enough so that there will be a gradual loss of brake fluid. He leaves town the next day and is on his way to Myrtle Beach when her car careens off a winding mountain road, bursts into flames, and she dies. The ensuing fire covers up the small nick in the brake lines.

He moves to the beach where the weather is warm and prey abounds. He figures most of the women are rich and looking to have a good time. Instead of living off the land, he will now live off the bodies and wealth of rich women.

Chapter 2: Mickke D

It is Monday morning and the sun hangs low in a sky bruised with storm clouds. I am in my office on Sea Mountain Highway, not far from the beach, in the Cherry Grove section of North Myrtle Beach, South Carolina.

My cell phone rings. "Mickke D Real Estate. How can I help you?"

"Hey Mickke D, it's Cathy Jay. How are you?"

A voice from out of the past. "Well hey yourself Miss Cathy; long time no see, no talk. Are you calling to show one of my listings?"

"I wish. No, this doesn't have anything to do with real estate. One of my closest girlfriends is missing, and I was told you may be able to find her for me."

Cathy is around 60 years old and fifteen years my senior. We worked for the same real estate company when I first got my license. She has been in the business for a long time and helped me learn the ropes when I first started.

"I think you need to call the police, Cathy. How long has she been missing?"

"I figure at least a week. I have not seen or heard from her since a week ago last Saturday night, and I already called the police. They went over to her condo and looked around. Her car is gone and they think she just went on vacation and didn't tell anyone."

"Well, you know that could be a possibility."

"I don't think so. If she were going away, she would have called me and let me know."

I think for a minute. "Okay, give me her name and I'll look into it for you. Who told you to call me about a missing person?"

"I spoke with Detective Concile at the police station and she suggested I call you. She said you do investigative work on the side."

I do own a company called Grand Strand Investigations. I inherited the company from a guy who tried to kill me, oddly enough. My neighbor, Jim Bolin, who just like me is from Ohio and a die-hard Ohio State fan, runs the company for me. He does the brunt of the work and I only help him out when he gets in a bind. The business is located in the same building as my landscape business and real estate office.

"Okay Cathy, let me see what I can find out and I'll get back to you."

જ~જ

I walk down the hall toward Jim's office. As I pass the reception desk, I smile at Beverly, my receptionist and part-time girlfriend. She returns my smile with eyebrows lifted in cold disdain. We have good months and bad months. She says I lack commitment. I say it's because I have been married, divorced, and broke three times. And since I am financially well off at the present time, I don't plan to share half or more of it with a fourth wife.

Jim is in his office looking through some file folders. Jim is a retired FBI special staff agent. He is 55 years old, a big, strong, tough, good-looking guy who always has a smile on his face and loves to play golf. He spends about three days a week in the office, depending on the weather and if he is able to get a tee time.

"Hey big guy, what do you have going on?" I say as I walk in.

"Oh, I'm still trying to find Senator Brazile's missing employee. I don't understand why he is so concerned about a missing secretary."

"Maybe there's more to it than the senator is telling you," I offer.

Jim looks over the top of his glasses. "I think you're right and I'm going to keep searching."

"By the way Jim, do you have time to look into another missing person for me?"

He shakes his head. "Not right now, maybe in a week or two. Who's missing?"

"Oh, just a friend of a friend of mine in real estate," I answer.

"Did they call the police?"

"Yes, she did and Detective Concile referred her to us."

Jim answers with a mischievous grin, "Well, if I were you, I would call your friend Detective Concile and ask her why she did that."

"As a matter of fact Jim, I was just about to do that. Good luck with Senator Brazile's missing secretary."

I was hoping to get Jim to look into this for me but I guess I'll have to do this investigation myself, which should not be a problem. I spent two years as an investigative officer with Army JAG at Fort Bragg. I guess I'm just not real gung-ho about doing it because the last time I investigated something I ended up getting shot at and almost killed. But then again, how difficult can it be to find a missing person?

As I venture back past Beverly's desk, I try smiling and waving this time. I get a tart wave and eyes flashing with irritation from Beverly and not even a hint of a smile or compromise. Beverly has a fine body with long, blond hair and beautiful long legs. She is almost ten years younger than I am. I met her by chance while walking my dog Blue on the beach one day about four months ago.

We were getting along pretty well until the other day when I went to pick her up for dinner. She was waiting outside the check-in area at Tillman Resort and when she got into my 81' Corvette, she handed me a present. She said to go ahead and open it before we go to dinner. The gift was rather small and wrapped in bright red paper with a white bow. I opened the package and I found bright red men's bikini underwear. "What the hell is this?" I blurted without thinking. I'd had a previous experience with red boxer shorts that didn't go well.

She quickly answered, "What does it look like? It's red bikini underwear. I thought you would look cute in them."

Again, I opened my mouth and inserted my foot. "You know I only wear boxers, and my God, it looks like something a skinny Santa Claus would wear."

With eyes glaring and lips pursed she replied, "Well, I'll tell you what. Why don't you lose some weight and wear them on Christmas or better yet, stick them where ...." She didn't finish her thought. She got out, slammed the door to my pristine Corvette, and went back inside the complex. I closed my eyes and shuddered as the door slammed. I checked the electric window to make sure it was still working. We haven't had dinner, lunch, or anything else since. I think this is going to be one of those bad months.

Once I get back at my desk, I put a call into Detective Sam Concile. I first met Sam when an assassin tried to burn down my office. Later she was the lead detective at two unrelated shootings which took place at my house. Sam is a bleached blonde in her mid-forties and seems like a very efficient detective. She does need a class in how to smile every once in a while.

She answers on the first ring. "Detective Concile, its Mickke D. How are you today?"

"Mickke D, what have you done now? Shot someone, blown something up, or burned something down? In addition, I'm still not sure about that cargo ship which sank off the coast of Pawleys Island. I just know you had something to do with that also."

"Nice to hear from you too, detective. I haven't done anything wrong. I'm just calling to ask why you referred Cathy Jay to GSI."

She hesitates and then replies, "Oh, you mean that missing persons case?"

"Yes, that's the one."

She hesitates again. "Her name was Ellen something. We checked out her condo and talked to all the neighbors. Her car was gone and it looked like she just went on vacation and forgot to tell anyone."

"So then why the referral?"

"Miss Jay was adamant that her friend wouldn't leave without telling her or at least calling her and since she was in real estate, I thought of you."

"And good thoughts they were, I'll bet."

"Yeah, right. Just remember, most of those cases where you were involved are still open."

"Thanks, detective. I'll remember that."

I have the impression she is just messing with me. If she really thought I was some sort of a criminal, why would she refer the case to GSI? On the other hand, was there something she wasn't telling me?

I dig a little deeper. "So detective, is that the end of your investigation? You concluded she went on vacation?"

"I did a little more checking, but as far as I am concerned, it is. I figure that is about as much information as I am going to get."

Now I am confused. It's as if she wants to tell me more but she is not sure if she should. "Look detective, if GSI is going to look into this missing persons case for you, which is what I think you want, I am going to need everything you have learned up to this point in the investigation."

"Okay, Mickke D, but this is off the record. It did not come from me."

"Okay, off the record, go ahead," I answer quickly.

"Do you know what a cougar is?"

"Sure, it's a large brown cat that lives in the mountains."

"No, I mean a female cougar."

"Of course, it's a large brown female cat that lives in the mountains."

"Very funny. A cougar is defined as a female over forty who dates a male at least eight years younger than her."

"Oh, that kind of cougar. Do they really exist? I thought that was just an old wives' tale."

I can hear a smile in her voice as she answers, "Oh yes, they exist big time here at the beach. But they are very discreet and almost a closed society."

"And what does this have to do with Ellen?" I ask.

"You could say, from what little bit of information I have been able to gather, Ellen was the queen of the cougars."

"Why did you say that in the past tense, do you think she is dead?"

"I don't know, but right now no one is going to talk to the police, so unless we find a body, she turns up, or you are able to gather some information on your own, my investigation is at a standstill."

"Okay, thanks for the information, detective. I'll get back to Cathy and see what I can find out."

Before I can end the call she says, "Remember Mickke D, if you find out anything, be sure and let me know."

"Of course, you'll be the first person I call."

Chapter 3: Ellen

Ellen Thorn moved to the beach almost eight years ago from Northern Ohio. Her husband of twenty-five years died unexpectedly from a massive heart attack, and two months after the funeral she was on her way south. She'd had enough of the cold, overcast, dreary winters along with the rain, snow, and ice next to the shores of Lake Erie.

Now she is sixty years old, slim with a great body, and can dance the legs off a man half her age. She has beauty that has faded little since her youth. She owns a condo on the ocean, is filthy rich, and loves to shag dance. She does not flaunt her wealth and everyone, particularly the men, seem to like her. Among her close, tight circle of friends, she is known as the "Cougar Queen." Where some women are afraid to make the first move if they see a man they are interested in, Ellen is not. Her philosophy is you can't be a winner if you don't play the game. She has no problem making the first move. She figures it's like buying a new pair of shoes: try them on and if they don't feel good and they don't look good on you, don't buy them.

She has had several boyfriends since her move to Myrtle Beach, the majority of them younger, and most of them have fulfilled the wants, needs, and desires that her late husband had not taken the time to do. He was always too busy working a stressful job, hence the heart attack. She had grown very tired of that way of life.

Her latest "friend" Jack is working out extremely well for her. He is a great dancer and has the most magical fingers of any man she has ever met. They sizzle on her body like cold raindrops on a hot metal roof. He always does what she wants, when she wants.

There is only one problem with Jack. After several months of fun and pleasure in the sun, she receives an unexpected monetary request from him.

Because of her wealth, she knows there are men out there who would try to take advantage of her, so she knows a sham when she hears one. Jack comes to her and wants to borrow $100,000 for six months. He says he has found a foolproof investment where he can easily double his money and that he is willing to pay her $5,000 in interest for that six-month period. He says he does not have that amount in liquid cash and it would take weeks to get his money out of trusts and CDs. This sends red danger signals blinking through her brain. She tells him she will consider the request and let him know. Her next move was a background check, and decides to do a background check on all of her "new friends" before she starts a relationship. Especially after a bad experience not too long ago with a strange man. She is not into kinky sex and that guy was about three fries short of a happy meal. She ditched that guy in a hurry. She should have learned from that experience.

Once she receives the background information, she realizes that everything Jack had told her about himself had been a lie. He not only is not the person she thought he was, he had spent time in prison on a fraud conviction. She plans to tell him that their affair is over. She will make it very clear to him that she never wants to see or hear from him again.

She sets up a dinner with Jack at Filet's next to the swing bridge in North Myrtle Beach, Sunday night at 7:00.

Chapter 4: The Hunter Arrives

Once the hunter arrives in Myrtle Beach, he leases a golf course condo for six months at Crow Creek Golf Course, which is just over the line in North Carolina. He wants to see if he is going to like living at the beach before buying a home or condo. His biggest hurdle to overcome is the heat and humidity. It was warm in Colorado during the summer but the humidity was always low.

He knows nothing about golf but he acquires a job as a bag attendant at Oyster Bay, which is not far from where he is living. He only works three days a week for minimum wage plus tips. He makes more off the tips than his wages. His job is to smile a lot, talk nice, and remove golf bags from vehicles and put them on the bag stand. He also loads the golf bags onto the golf carts and sometimes takes members' clubs out to their cars for them.

The nice thing about his job is that he meets quite a few available women. A lot of women play golf in the Myrtle Beach area. He has learned to ask specific questions to certain women and wait for the right response.

"So ma'am how did you play today?" he will ask.

"Oh, not very well but thank you for asking," she usually replies.

"Maybe you need a golf lesson. I know someone who may be able to help you."

"Would that someone be you, by chance?"

"Oh no, not me. I don't even play golf. The only way I could ever help such a lovely lady like you would be to take her to dinner sometime."

If she answers, "I just may take you up on that, young man," he then gets real smooth. "I don't want to sound pushy so why don't I just give you my number and if you're available some weekend, give me a call."

If she is interested she usually comes back with, "How sweet of you, I'm available this weekend and here is my number. Call me."

He will of course call and sometimes the dinner will lead to other things, like coffee at her place. He never has any women friends over to his place. He doesn't want anyone to know where he lives. Now if there were just some way to get them back for a second date. Second dates are very rare for him. Maybe he is too rough with them the first time. However, he likes it rough, so if they don't come back for more, he figures it's their loss.

Chapter 5: The Confrontation

Ellen tells Jack when they first sit down to dinner at Filet's that they can discuss his request after they leave the restaurant. She wants to make sure he does not try to stick her with the dinner check.

Jack is his usual charming self during dinner. He even rubs his beach sandal-covered foot up and down her leg under the table, which sends hot flashes up and down her spine. She thinks that maybe she should just wait until after "dessert" at her place tonight to tell him the bad news, but cooler heads prevail. No, she needs to end this right now.

The sky has turned from dusk to the color of faded ink by the time they get to the parking lot. There are few cars in the parking area and not a person is in sight as they reach Ellen's car, which is located in an out of the way parking area.

Jack says in a coy voice, "Do you want me to meet you at your place or do you want to go to my place?"

Before Ellen has a chance to answer, a dark figure steps from behind the car parked next to hers. He is dressed in black and has a Richard Nixon Halloween mask covering his face. His voice is hard to understand, as if he has a mouth full of marbles.

"Unlock the car and both of you get in the front seat. Disobey and I will shoot both of you right here."

Both of them notice a gun in the man's hand. Jack feigns bravery. "Look, if you want money you can have everything we have. Just let us go."

"Do as I say and you won't get hurt. I only want the car."

"Take the damn car. We won't say a word," Jack replies. He doesn't care because it's Ellen's car, not his.

The man in black cocks his weapon. Ellen and Jack both recognize the sound. They get into the front seat of Ellen's car. The hunter slides into the back seat behind Ellen.

Chapter 6: The Condo

After speaking with Detective Concile, I call Cathy back. "Cathy, do you have a key to Ellen's condo? I would like to look around."

"Yes I do, when would you like to see it?"

"You know where my office is on Sea Mountain Highway. Come on down whenever you're available, the sooner the better."

She answers quickly. "I'll be there in about thirty minutes."

Since I have a tee time this afternoon, if it doesn't rain, and I am not sure how long this will take, I follow Cathy in my vehicle to Ellen's condo. She tells me it is a gated building so to stay close and just follow her in. The building is very bland in appearance. It is located directly on the ocean, is eight stories high, which does not include the first two floors that are used for parking. You need a key to get in the gate, a key for the elevator, and a key to open any door on any floor if you walk up instead of taking the elevator. As a real estate broker, I would classify it as a very secure building.

Ellen's condo is a penthouse unit located on the top floor. There are four units on each floor, two corner units and two inside units. On the top floor, there are only two penthouse condos that aren't much to look at from the outside but the inside is a completely different story. Cathy tells me the unit is almost 2,700 heated square feet with three bedrooms and three full baths. The living area or great room is massive. It has a vaulted ceiling and the wall facing the ocean is ceiling-to-floor glass with an oversized set of beautiful glass French doors. They blend right in with the glass walls leading out to the balcony, which has to be eight feet wide. Probably ten feet of the corner wall located in the kitchen is also glass and the balcony wraps all the way around. A majestic, breathtaking ocean view is blanketed before my eyes from anywhere in the living area or kitchen. I have shown quite a few ocean-front condos but this one has to be in the top five I've seen.

We start our tour in the kitchen, which is very large with granite countertops and all stainless steel appliances. A small table sits against the glass wall so one could have breakfast inside and still have a gorgeous view of the ocean. Our next stop is the master bedroom. Cathy tells me the bedroom is 25 feet by 20 feet and again the wall facing the ocean is all glass with a sliding glass door out to an extension of the living room balcony. The master bath is huge with a double shower and an over-sized Jacuzzi tub. I count six showerheads in the shower, two in the ceiling and two on each end. I am impressed.

The other two bedrooms are regular size and the other two baths are nice but not like the master bath. All of the floors in the condo, except for the two guest bedrooms, which have Berber carpeting, are an off-white Italian tile.

After the tour, we go back to the living room and sit on the burgundy red leather couch. "This place is spotless. Does it always look this nice?" I ask, staring out at the beautiful blue Atlantic. I picture myself sitting in my La-Z-Boy just staring at the ocean and maybe reading a book. Actually, with this view, I may even consider writing a book.

Cathy breaks my train of thought with her answer. "She has a cleaning lady come in once a week, and yes, it always looks this way."

I start to get the feeling that I'm missing something right here in plain sight. I get up and walk around. I go back into the master bedroom and then walk through the kitchen again. I was right. I see the one thing that shouldn't be there if she is that particular and was going on vacation. The coffeemaker has a full pot of coffee in it. I look closer; it is on auto. If she were planning to go away, why would she have the coffeemaker set to make coffee the following morning? Did she forget or did she not make it home for morning coffee?

I ask Cathy, "Would she have left the coffeemaker on if she were going on vacation? Could she have forgotten?"

"No way," Cathy promptly answers.

I'm beginning to think Cathy may be right. Ellen could be a missing person. I opt not to call Detective Concile until I get some substantial evidence that there may have been foul play involved.

I thank Cathy for the tour and tell her that I will contact her the minute I learn something. I make it to River Hills and meet Jim for golf. I don't play very well because I keep thinking about that gorgeous condo and what could have happened to Ellen Thorn.

Chapter 7: The Hunter and Jack

Ellen and Jack had a lot of bad luck that fateful evening, but most of it can be attributed to Jack. The hunter stopped to have a beer in North Myrtle Beach. He usually goes to small, out of the way, oceanfront bars where occasionally he may pick up a woman. He likes to stay away from the Crow Creek and the Oyster Bay area in North Carolina where he lives and works.

He is having second thoughts about his move to the beach. It has been a real culture shock to him so far. Everyone back in Colorado seemed to be working, liked to hunt and fish, and was not very rich. Here everyone he meets is retired, not working, and very well off, at least they give the impression of being well off. He is having a rough time making the adjustment from almost a reclusive way of life to being out in the public with lots of people. However, if he wants to meet women, he has no choice. They are not going to come knocking on his door. He also has discovered there are quite a few men out for the same thing as him, to hustle some rich divorced woman or widow. There seems to be constant competition for the best-looking and richest women. Of course, the women love it. Some good-looking, younger man is constantly hitting on them.

The hunter takes a seat at the end of the bar and surveys the room. It is a normal bar and grill setting, a long "L" shaped bar with several tables positioned nearby. Most of the patrons are sitting out on the patio where clear plastic walls protect them from the cool ocean breeze. All of the women seem to be with someone so he forgets about going into "pick-up" mode.

He can't help but notice a man, four chairs away from him, who is bending the bartender's ear. He has probably had one too many and therefore he is talking much louder than he normally would.

Jack is telling Andy, the bartender, what he thinks is a good luck story.

"Yeah Andy, I am finally going to collect some big bucks from that rich broad I have been dating."

Andy asks with a smile and a thick German accent, "How did you manage dat, Jack?"

"It is just my good looks and charm, Andy."

Andy continues to grin. "Come on Jack, if you mean dat Ellen Thorn lady, I thought she vas smarter dan dat."

"Yes, she's the one. They call her the Cougar Queen. I'm having dinner with her Sunday night at Filet's around seven and after dessert at my place, it will be jackpot time."

"Vell Jack, after your big payoff, are you going to pay your bar tab?" Andy asks.

"As a matter of fact Andy, I'm going to pay you before I leave today because the day after I get paid, I'm out of here."

The hunter looks up from his beer, stares directly at Jack, and asks, "So how much are you getting, Jack?"

Andy and Jack, both surprised by the intervention, turn and look the hunter's way. Jack tartly replies, "What's it to you buddy? I wasn't talking to you. But since you asked, I'm getting a hundred large. Now mind your own business." Most men would not have mentioned the amount, but Jack loves to brag.

The hunter gives Jack a stern stare but does not reply. He goes back to sipping on his beer. He keeps his face turned away from Jack because he can feel it turning bright red. His insides are churning. He feels like a volcano about to erupt. He finally chugs the rest of his beer, throws some bills on the bar, and leaves.

He goes directly to his pick-up truck and opens the glove compartment. He pulls out his 9mm Luger 23 and his first thought is to go back in the bar, put the gun in Jack's mouth and pull the trigger. What an asshole. He sits in his truck and takes several deep breaths. He decides he should be more upset with Ellen than with Jack.

The hunter had gone out with Ellen one time and got absolutely nowhere. She actually referred to him as a pervert and gave him the impression he was not good enough for her. And now she is going to give this lowlife Jack one hundred thousand dollars? "We'll see about that," he mutters to himself.

Chapter 8: The Sky Wheel

Beverly decides to call a truce and asks me to take her down to the new boardwalk in Myrtle Beach for a walk, a ride on the Sky Wheel after dark and then dinner at Jimmy Buffet's LandShark Restaurant, which is located at the base of the Sky Wheel. I pick her up about 6 p.m. in the Trailblazer, not the Corvette, and this time she does not come to the car bearing gifts. I was prepared to accept any gift cordially and keep my big mouth shut.

On the way to Myrtle Beach, Beverly fills me in on the Sky Wheel specs, which she says she got from the internet. I listen and nod my head, but I really don't care. It's just a big Ferris wheel. She tells me the Sky Wheel sits 200 feet above sea level and is the only observation wheel of its kind in the U.S. It has forty-two climate-controlled Swiss-manufactured fully enclosed gondolas and every night spices up the sky with an LED lightshow. Again, I just nod my head and smile. She turns her head and gives me an angry stare.

Since this is the off-season in Myrtle Beach, it is easy to find a parking spot close to the north end of the boardwalk. We no sooner set foot on the boardwalk before we see the Sky Wheel lit up like a huge revolving Christmas tree. It is blue, green, red, and white and then it begins flashing and changing colors. It looks like a cross between a fireworks display and a laser light show. I have to admit, although not to Beverly, it is a very impressive sight.

Suddenly my mind leaves the beauty of the Sky Wheel. My former Special Forces and investigative officer training notices four unsavory individuals resting their backsides against the railing of the boardwalk not too far from the entrance to the walkway going out to the Pier 14 Restaurant. They see us about the same time and tap each other on the arms. There is no one else in sight except them and us. I learned a long time ago that my five senses are in service to my sixth sense, which is the intuitive sense of danger to body and soul. I normally would not be that concerned but since Beverly is with me, I am a little bit apprehensive.

I touch my back where my blue jeans begin and touch the handle of my chrome-plated .45, which my beach shirt conceals. I feel a whole lot better all of a sudden. I carry the gun because years ago, a Colombian cartel kingpin put a reward on my head and not too long ago someone tried to collect. That person is now dead but I have a funny feeling the reward is still in effect. Just the other day, I had that uneasy feeling that someone was watching me.

I say softly to Beverly, "If those guys say anything to us, just ignore them and keep walking."

"No problem," she quickly replies as if she is not the least bit concerned.

As we near their location, the head gang member takes a step forward and spits on the boardwalk. His voice has an intimidating sound to it. "Hey pops, how would you like to donate your valuables and money to our boys club, and maybe your hot bitch would like to donate her body as well?"

What did he call me, "pops"? And he called Beverly a hot bitch. Hot maybe, but not a bitch.

Before I can calm down enough to answer, Beverly says, "Mickke D, let me take care of this, these gentlemen do not understand the situation here."

The head gang member laughs. "Mickke D, cute name, I'll take fries with my burger, pops." He turns toward the other three gang members and stares. As if on cue, they burst out laughing.

There, he called me "pops" again. Now I am really getting upset. I can feel my old demons beginning to snarl deep inside my gut.

Beverly takes a step closer to the gang member. With droll on his lips, he says to her, "So bitch, would you like some lovin' from a real man?"

Her mouth turns down and she laughs softly. "Look at me, dickhead, I piss sitting down, so I doubt if I'm your type."

His eyes flash with irritation and rage. "Why, you no good........" Before he can finish his thought, she winds up, does a roundhouse kick and catches him beside the ear. He crumbles to the boardwalk as if all the air was just let out of his balloon. He lies motionless on the screwed-in wooden planks.

The next thing I hear is three clicks and I notice the other three have switchblade knives drawn and flashing. I can see the colored lights of the Sky Wheel reflecting on the shiny blades.

It's as if I'm moving and thinking in slow motion. I look at Beverly and think "who are you and what have you done with my significant other?" Beverly always seemed so quiet and introspective, except maybe the night she slammed the door of my Corvette. This can't be the same woman.

I come back to reality, pull the .45 from my back and hold it down at my side, not aimed at them, but in plain view of the three who are trying to look like tough gang members. "Didn't your mothers ever tell you never take a knife to a gun fight? Now drop the knives or I will drop you. Who wants to die first?"

The next thing I hear is the sound of three knives hitting the boardwalk. All three raise their hands without me asking them to do so and turn around. I'll bet they have done this before. They seem to know the drill.

"Leave the knives, pick up your friend, and get the hell out of here. I'm going to guess the cops are on their way."

Within seconds, they are gone, disappearing over the dunes and onto the beach, dragging their still groggy leader.

My gaze returns to Beverly. "Where did you learn that move?"

In an almost embarrassed tone of voice, she answers, "Oh, it's nothing; I've taken a few self-defense classes."

Self-defense classes my ass, the move she put on that joker took years of training. The timing has to be perfect and your foot needs to be hard as a rock. She never even flinched after delivering the blow to his head.

She notices me thinking. "Well, are you ready to continue our evening? Do you want to ride, walk, or eat first?"

It's as if absolutely nothing just happened. My first thought is whatever we do, I am not going to do anything to upset her. She may beat the crap out of me.

Before I can answer, over Beverly's shoulder I notice two police officers on bikes coming from the direction of the Sky Wheel. I suppose someone in one of the restaurants noticed the commotion and called the police. I return my weapon to its holstered location in the small of my back.

They pull up beside us and ask if there is a problem.

"No problem officers, there were what looked like some teenage gang members here with big mouths, but we bluffed them and they ran," I replied, not quite sure how to answer their question.

"And did the teenage gang members have switch-blade knives?"

I look down at the boardwalk where the officer is looking and reply, "Yes they did but I talked them in to dropping them."

He looks me up and down and asks, "Are any of these gang members hurt?"

"Well, I don't think so, although one of them will probably have a headache in the morning."

The officers look at each other. "Let me see some ID from both of you."

Beverly quickly flashes a big grin, sighs, and answers, "Sorry officer, I left my purse locked in the trunk. We were planning a nice walk on the boardwalk, a ride on the Sky Wheel, and dinner at LandShark."

The officer's gaze shifts toward me. "What about you, did you lock your ID in the trunk also?"

"No officer, here is my driver's license and business card."

"Grand Strand Investigations. So you're a PI, Mr. MacCandlish?"

"Well sort of, I own the company but someone else does most of the work."

Again, the two officers look at each other. "Do you want to file any type of a complaint against these gang members?"

"No, I don't think so, officers. We're fine and they learned a good lesson tonight."

"And what lesson is that Mr. MacCandlish?"

I turn and look at Beverly. "Be careful who you mouth off to."

The officer hands me back my ID and gives me his card. He says that if we change our minds to give him a call.

Beverly and I continue our jaunt. We ride the Sky Wheel and have one of the most delicious foot-long hotdogs I've ever tasted at the LandShark Restaurant. Beverly had hers plain but I had chili on mine. We take a short walk after eating and then head back to the Trailblazer. It is very dark so I keep my eyes watching in all directions, just in case Beverly's victim decides to visit again. We don't encounter any of the gang members but again, I feel like someone is watching us.

Chapter 9: The Swamp

The hunter puts his weapon against the back of Ellen's head and tells her to drive out Route 9 toward Loris and to not speed if she wants to continue breathing. As soon as they are across the swing bridge, Jack asks, "What are you planning to do with us?"

"If you must know, numb nuts, I am going to leave you out in a swamp somewhere so that it will take you a long time to get back to civilization."

Jack sheepishly asks another question. "Aren't there alligators and snakes in the swamp?"

The hunter almost laughs aloud. "Yes, there are, Jack. I would be very careful if I were you. By the way, give me your cell phones. I don't want you to be discovered too soon."

Ellen and Jack hand over their cell phones without any further questions. They drive out Route 9, cross under Highway 31, go through the intersection of Highway 57, pass Colonial Charters, Aberdeen, Long Bay and finally the hunter tells Ellen to turn right across from the entrance to Myrtle Lakes North. They drive back on the dirt road about two miles and then he tells her to turn left onto what seems to be no more than a wide dirt path into a swampy forest and to drive slowly. The farther they go, the darker it becomes and the path becomes wetter and only a one-lane path. Billybob Swamp is pulling them into the bowels of its lair.

The hunter points his weapon and says, "Turn right at that big tree and pull down to the edge of the water. Turn off the headlights, roll down the back windows, put the car in park, and leave the engine running."

"Do you want us to get out now?" Jack struggles to ask. He has already decided that the minute he steps outside the car, he is going to run and take his chances with the swamp instead of waiting to see what the man with the gun is going to do. Ellen can fend for herself.

"No, not yet," the hunter replies as he takes off his mask. "First, I want both of you to turn around and look at me."

Ellen looks surprised and says between sobs, "Oh my God, that voice, I know you, you're ….."

Before she has a chance to say his name, the hunter responds, "Yes, you're right, Ellen, and Jack knows me too, don't you, Jack?"

"You sound like the guy from the bar the other day. Hey, if I said anything out of line, it was probably because I had too much to drink."

The hunter replies calmly; the three peppermint mints he had in his mouth have melted, "Yes, Jack you were a complete ass-hole. You should not have bragged about how much money Ellen was going to give you tonight and that as soon as you got paid you planned to leave town."

Ellen looks at Jack and in between sobs says, "You bastard, I was not going to give you a penny."

Jack looks surprised and puzzled and then he says to the hunter, "So there, does that make everything all right? She was not going to give me anything."

"No, it doesn't Jack, open your mouth," the hunter sort of whispers and as Jack slowly opens wide he shoves the gun in his mouth. Jack can taste the gun oil used to clean the weapon and he begins to choke. He pees his pants.

"Oh, and by the way Jack, I lied to you about letting you go." The hunter pulls the trigger and splatters the back of Jack's head all over a now-shattered, passenger-side window.

Ellen screams and wets her pants. She tries to unbuckle her seatbelt and to get her door open but to no avail. The hunter grabs her by her hair, yanks her head back and puts the hot barrel of the gun in her ear. She screams again but the swamp envelopes the noise and no response is heard.

"Ellen, you treated me like a dog," the hunter snarls between gritted teeth, as his breathing grows short and sharp, almost hissing with fury. "You are as bad as my ex-wife and I killed her also." Ellen's eyes double in size as she starts to scream. With eyes flashing and nostrils flaring with rage, he pulls the trigger and splatters the side of her head all over the driver's side door and shattered window.

The hunter calmly gets out of the back seat, opens both rear doors, and then opens Ellen's door. He unbuckles her seatbelt and shoves her lifeless bloody body into the middle toward the console. He places his foot on the brake and pulls the gearshift into drive. He closes her door and backs away as the car slowly moves into the swampy lake. The car disappears under the dark, brackish water. Air bubbles begin to rise to the surface as the car sinks deeper into the swamp. The bubbles quickly evaporate into the heavy, moist air. Before long, it's as if the car never existed. He takes their cell phones from his pocket and throws them into the water. Billybob Swamp has claimed two victims, probably never to be heard from again.

He picked this spot after fishing with a man who also works at the golf course. The man said the water was between ten and twelve feet deep in this area; more than deep enough to hide the car. He figures by having the rear doors open and the windows down, since there are alligators around, they will eventually eliminate any evidence of the bodies.

He takes a small hand towel out of his pocket, wipes off the gun, and puts it in his waistband. He takes off his blood-spattered gloves and places them, along with the towel, into a plastic bag. He puts on new gloves. He takes a small, high-beam flashlight from another pocket and walks toward the soggy path where they turned in from the dirt road. He finds a large pile of pine boughs and other limbs and begins to remove them.

Under the limbs and brush, he finds his Harley Davidson motorcycle which he left earlier in the day. He had brought it out on a trailer hitched to his pickup truck, covered with a tarp sitting between two wooden horses, which he found in the maintenance building at the golf course. When he left, the tarp was covering only the two horses on the trailer, the bike left behind and concealed. If anyone noticed him, it would have looked as if he came out with the same thing he had brought in. A small rake is attached to his bike with bungee cords. He takes the rake and removes any sign of tire tracks or footprints from the sandy edge of the water. He pushes the bike out to the path and then rakes that area.

He opens the saddlebags on the bike, gets out his leather jacket, and puts it on along with his helmet. He doesn't turn his headlight on until he gets out to the dirt road. He sees no other vehicles or people until he gets back to Route 9. He rides back to Filet's where his pickup truck and trailer are waiting for him. He drives the bike onto the trailer, covers it with the tarp and drives back to Crow Creek.

The hunter is elated; this was his first hunt since killing the cougar, the rabbit, and his ex-wife in Colorado. He had planned every step of the attack and it was a complete success. He can't wait to go hunting again. The feeling was almost on the same level as sex. Before going to bed, he starts a list of women who never came back for a second date or turned him down for a first date. He decides to stay around Myrtle Beach for a while longer. He is starting to enjoy living at the beach.

Chapter 10: The Office

As I pull into the parking lot at the office the next morning, there is a fine, misty rain drizzling down, muting the views of the ocean-front condos and resorts. Jim's car is already there; he doesn't enjoy playing golf in the rain. That's good because I need him to look into Beverly's background for me. I gaze in my rear view mirror and notice my bloodshot, burning eyes look as if I am suffering from a three-day hangover, which is not the case. After spending several hours at Beverly's place last night and the episode at the boardwalk, I was bushed and keyed up when I finally got home. I couldn't sleep and then Blue, a German Shepherd/husky mix that I rather inherited from my ex-neighbor, wanted out twice during the night. Every time I started to fall back asleep, I kept remembering a quote I once read in a book. *Evil could masquerade as beauty, that black hearts were sometimes clothed in compassion, that evil didn't have a calling card alerting everyone to its pending visit or shape.*

Beverly seemed to be the main, pending shape on my mind. It was not only her comment, *I've taken a few self-defense classes,* but also most of my recent relationships have not lasted very long, yet Beverly and I have been a couple for almost four months now. I can't help but wonder why. My other girlfriends said I was very difficult to be around after a few dates. I don't feel as if I have changed my attitude toward women, that I am treating Beverly the same way I treated my other girlfriends and ex-wives, so why is she still here? I told her in the beginning that I was not looking for a permanent relationship and she seemed fine with that, although she does occasionally mention the "commitment" word. Oh well, let me see what Jim can find out.

I look around before entering the building. I still have the feeling someone is watching me. As I wave at Beverly, her eyes light up and her face softens. She has a big smile on her face, which she should after last night. She seems to be over her misgivings with me. I go directly to Jim's office and close the door behind me.

"Jim, I need you to see what your friends at the Bureau can find out about Beverly."

He peers over the top of his glasses with a look of puzzlement. "Why would you want to check on her? I thought you two were getting along pretty well considering your luck with women."

I tell him about the episode at the boardwalk and that I really don't know a whole lot about her.

Jim shakes his head and says, "Personally, I think you're becoming paranoid, but okay, give me her full name and whatever you do know about her, and I'll see what I can find out for you."

"Well, her name is Beverly S. Beery; she's around thirty-five years old. She told me she was born and raised in Jacksonville, Illinois, went to college at a private girls school and worked as a computer analyst for Caterpillar Industries in Chicago. She supposedly now has a private computer service, which she runs out of her condo when she's not working here in the office.

"And speaking of paranoid, I keep thinking someone is watching me. Have you noticed any strange people around the office lately or any strange cars in the parking lot?"

"No, not really."

I thank Jim and ask him to call me when he finds out something.

෧᳞෧

Around 11:30, Jim calls and wants to know if I'm available for lunch. I tell him sure and that we'll go over to R.W. Woods for lunch.

As we pass Beverly's desk, she asks, "What are you guys up to?"

"We're going to lunch and then we're going down to the PGA Superstore in North Myrtle Beach. Jim wants me to check out some new clubs he is thinking about buying. I'll see you later."

Normally I would ask her to go along, but I think we may be discussing her at lunch. She gets this hurt little girl look on her face and says, "Have fun, maybe I'll call Jannie to see if she wants to have lunch today."

Jannie is the wife of Mark Yale, who runs my landscape business, which is also located in the building. Mark is an ex-Green Beret who was with me in the jungles of Colombia many years ago.

&∝⋖

R.W. Woods is located at the corner of Highway 90 and Sea Mountain Highway, which used to be the only route into the beach. I've heard stories about how the cars would back up for miles waiting for the swing bridge to open. This was long before the big new bridge was built over the waterway. The restaurant began as a general store, which R.W. opened in 1960. The owners then turned it into a full-fledged restaurant in 2001. They're only open for breakfast and lunch and you had better get there before noon or you will be standing in line. R.W. and his wife Louise along with their son Richard run the business and it's one of those friendly local places with a great atmosphere. The floors are the original wood and there is sports memorabilia everywhere. My only problem is that they have an Ohio State helmet on display, but it is hidden over in the corner at the end of a shelf. If you're not a South Carolina Gamecock or Clemson Tiger in this part of the country, you're the enemy.

We walk up to the counter and Richard says, "Cheeseburger, all the way, fries, and a diet Pepsi, right?" I don't go there regularly but he always seems to remember what everyone orders.

"Right. Jim, you want the same?"

Jim replies, "Sounds good to me since you're buying," and looking at Richard he says, "Go Buckeyes."

Richard gives him a funny look and gives the order to the lunch cook.

We get a table on the far side of the room away from the mainstream lunch bunch. Jim quietly says, "Everything you told me about Beverly is true."

I feel somewhat relieved. "That's good news; however, you don't seem to be real thrilled about giving me good news."

He appears perplexed and finally says, "It's almost too perfect. The Bureau could find nothing about her except exactly what you told me, which is exactly what she told you. There was a birth certificate, college records, and employment records. If I were looking at her as a person of interest, I would see red flags everywhere."

Now I look perplexed. "I don't understand, what do you mean?"

"Mickke D, from the information I was given and how the records were presented, I would be thinking two possibilities, CIA or Witness Protection."

Louise brings our lunch over to us and we enjoy it without a lot of banter. I am very shocked by Jim's evaluation of Beverly. R.W. and Louise wish us well as we leave, and Richard waves. I wonder if the Ohio State helmet will be missing when I come back the next time. It is a quiet trip back to the office.

Chapter 11: The Senator's Secretary

Connie Smith is gazing soulfully out of her third-floor bedroom window in her rented condo, located on the beach on Grand Cayman Island. She watches as a low-slung, oppressive gray sky yields warm rain. A few drops of that warm rain are tapping on her windowpanes.

She has been living on Grand Cayman for the past six months, ever since she left Washington D.C., along with more than $800,000 she confiscated from North Carolina United States Senator R. Gene Brazile.

Connie was his private secretary and in her mind, she still does not feel as if she actually stole the money. It was untraceable, tainted money. She was just doing the senator a favor by taking it. She believes the senator was salting away the cash for his walking around money once he retired. She figures the senator referred to it as a contribution from his constituents but she looked at it as an illegal bribe. She took the money from a locked compartment in his desk and wrote a letter to the senator explaining why he should not pursue her and what she would do if he did. She has not heard a word from him or anyone else since she has been on Grand Cayman.

She thought she would enjoy living on Grand Cayman for a long time but the past six months have been rather lonely. She is getting the urge to return to the States, if only for a short visit. Her money is secure in a local bank, and she feels fairly safe here; however, she doesn't seem to trust anyone she meets in a social setting. She has no real friends and she is always looking over her shoulder to see if someone is watching her.

She spends a lot of time on her computer searching cities she might like to visit. She definitely will not go back to D.C. for fear of being recognized and she would like a place close to the ocean. The ocean has turned out to be her only real friend lately. She spends hours sitting on the beach, listening and watching the waves come and go, sipping a glass of red wine.

She goes to a wig store and purchases a dark black, long hair wig to cover her short, natural auburn hair. She also purchased large, dark-rimmed glasses with clear transitional lenses. Now when she gazes into her mirror, she sees a completely different person. This new person looks more like a non-descript schoolteacher than an ex-private secretary of a United States senator. No one will notice her, let alone recognize her.

After reviewing pages of propaganda written on the internet, she has narrowed her vacation search to Virginia Beach, Va.; Wilmington, N.C.; Myrtle Beach, S.C.; or Charleston, S.C. Virginia Beach seems too close to Washington D.C., Charleston does not have many nice beaches, and Wilmington does not seem to push any hot buttons for her. That leaves Myrtle Beach as her vacation destination. The internet shows hundreds of things to do and there are enough people so no one will notice her. She calls the airline and makes a reservation.

Chapter 12: New Evidence

The ride back to the office from R.W. Woods is quiet and unassuming. I am not sure how I am going to handle the situation with Beverly. I actually have no proof that she is anything but what she told me she was. I can almost go along with the Witness Protection theory. She could have been moved from the West Coast to the East Coast or from somewhere in between. The CIA side of the equation makes no sense to me. Why would anyone, let alone a woman from the CIA, want to be in my screwed-up, demon-filled life? Jim has no solid evidence, just a hunch. However, that hunch covers thirty years of investigative work with the FBI. Should I confront her with Jim's hunch, which will probably screw up my sex life for quite a while, or just take a wait-and-see attitude? I decide to keep my mouth shut for now, but I plan to be much more attentive and observant around her in the future.

Beverly is not at her desk when we enter the office but there is a note on her chair. *Jannie and I went to lunch, LOL.* I thank Jim for the info and go back to my office.

As soon as I sit down my cell phone rings. It's Cathy. "Mickke D, I have some more interesting news for you. Ellen's latest boyfriend is also missing."

"How do you know he's missing?" Before she has a chance to answer, I add, "Did you call Detective Concile and tell her? And, do you know his name and where he lives?"

Cathy is not sure which question to answer first. "His name is Jack Miller and he was renting a condo at Heather Glen in Little River. One of my girlfriends called me this morning. She was out to dinner last night and several of the people at the restaurant said they had not seen Jack since last Saturday night, which was also the last time anyone had seen Ellen. Several of the guys had called his cell phone about playing golf this week, but got no answer. And I thought I would call you before I call the police, since they weren't much help the last time."

"Cathy, what can you tell me about this Jack guy?"

"Not much. He considers himself a Don Juan with the ladies, but I never could see what Ellen saw in him. Maybe all of his attributes are hidden from view."

I laugh and tell Cathy to go ahead and call Detective Concile. Let her know what she thinks about Jack, but don't tell her she called me. I thank her and tell her I will get back to her.

I open my desk drawer and look around for my new PI license. Jim and I both applied and received them when we started GSI. I've never used mine. It looks very official and I hope it will open some doors for me.

The nice thing about Cathy's call is that it gets my mind off my dilemma with Beverly. As another way to get her off my mind, I figure I will take a ride out to Heather Glen and see what I can find out about Jack Miller before Detective Concile gets there, if she goes at all.

৵৶

Heather Glen is part of The Glens Group. It is a lovely golf course unspoiled by development. When you drive in from Highway 17, there are condos on the left at the entrance but they are located far away from the clubhouse. The course has some contours and elevation to it. The fairways abound with trees, not homes. I go to the office at the entrance, flash my PI license, and ask for the manager. In a few minutes, Ray Bonzai appears at the front desk and invites me into his office. Ray looks to be in his forties, short, and sort of reminds me of the Pillsbury Dough Boy with glasses.

I show him my PI license, hand him my GSI business card, and introduce myself. "Mr. Bonzai, do you know a Jack Miller? He is supposedly renting one of your condos."

He quickly answers, "Oh yeah, I know Jack. Seems like a nice enough guy. He is renting 3C in Building G. Has he done something wrong? He hasn't paid this month's rent yet, should I be concerned?"

I reply, "Well I don't know, I have been hired to look into the possibility that he could be a missing person."

"Wow, come to think of it, I haven't seen him in over a week. So what do you need from me?"

"Would you mind taking me over to his condo and letting me look around?"

He pauses for a couple of seconds. "Sure, no problem. Let me get the key."

We walk over to Building G and Ray knocks on the door several times. He puts the key in the lock and then turns to me. "You don't think he could be dead or anything, do you?"

"Well, if he is, we'll know once you open the door, Ray. The smell will knock you down."

Ray backs off, takes the key out of the lock, and hands it to me. "Here, you open it."

I turn the key and slowly crack open the door, waiting for the pungent smell of death to waffle through the small opening. No odors find their way to my sensitive nose. I've smelled death many times before and it is a smell you never forget and never get used to.

I turn to Ray, who is still backing up and teasingly say, "I think we're okay, do you want to go in first?"

"No thanks, you're doing fine. I'll bring up the rear." He stammers.

I loudly call out "hello" twice, which is what I do when I enter a house or condo I am showing to a real estate client. Ray jumps. "Why didn't you tell me you were going to do that? You scared the shit out of me."

As we enter the living area, I ask Ray, "Was this condo furnished by Mr. Miller or the owner?"

"Jack rented it furnished," Ray whispers, while peeking around me to get a better look.

I try to reassure him. "Ray, I think we're okay. No one answered my greeting. You're free to roam around, just don't touch anything."

Ray continues to shadow me as I walk into the master bedroom. I immediately notice several suitcases and garment bags lying on the bed. "Ray, when is Mr. Miller's lease up?"

"I think he has another six months left on his lease, why do you ask?"

"Well, it looks to me like he is either planning a long vacation or leaving town in a hurry. Look at these bags."

Ray looks at the bags, then at me. "I hope it's just a vacation or I will have to explain to the owner of this place why he hasn't paid his rent."

I continue looking around the condo with Ray following me like a new puppy. "Does he always keep the place looking this good all the time?" I think to myself, *compared to this place and Ellen's condo, my house looks like a pigsty.*

"He does a lot of entertaining with his lady friends so he wants to put on a good impression. Actually, he keeps it fairly clean himself but he does have a cleaning lady come in twice a month and clean the entire condo."

I look at Ray and ask, "How do you know so much about his personal life?"

He hesitates and looks around the room. "Oh, since I'm recently divorced, he has invited me over if there was a party going on. That's not against the law, is it?"

Ray jumps again as all of a sudden someone knocks hard on the partially open front door and yells, "This is the police, is there anyone in there?"

They come through the front door with guns drawn. Ray moves behind me and calls out, "it's okay, I'm the condo manager and this guy is a private investigator."

I recognize the first two through the door as Woolever and Stratten. Right behind them comes Detective Sam Concile. I can tell right away she is upset with me, again.

Without a hint of a smile, she says, "Well, if it isn't Mr. Mac-Candlish. What a lovely surprise to see you here."

"Nice to see you too, detective. I'm just following up on a lead for a client of mine."

Everyone holsters their weapons, which makes me feel a whole lot better. I get very nervous and insecure when someone points a gun at me. This time the feeling quickly passes.

"And what have you discovered so far?" she tartly asks.

"Now you know that's privileged information, detective. Can we talk in private for a minute?"

She points toward the front door. "Sure Mickke D, I can hardly wait to hear this one."

She asks Woolever and Stratten to look around the condo and find out who this other guy is, what he knows, and take a statement from him.

We step outside and I divulge what I found at Ellen's condo. She looks at me with a puzzled look on her face as if she is trying to remember the coffeemaker. She wants to know why I did not call her immediately with what may be new evidence in a missing persons case. I tell her I needed more evidence to be sure and that after seeing Jack Miller's condo, I figure she may have two missing persons to look for instead of just one.

She tells me I can leave but to please keep her in the loop if I discover anything else. In other words, keep on investigating but don't keep everything to myself. I can live with that. She was almost civil with me this time, but I still haven't seen her smile.

As I am leaving, I thank Ray, who is giving a statement to Woolever and Stratton, for his help. He waves and continues his interview.

Chapter 13: Friday Night

It's late Friday afternoon along the Grand Strand. The weather is cool, about 65 degrees, but the air is boiling with anticipation. The movers and shakers along with the predators and cougars are getting ready for a night out on the town. The movers and shakers will be making a stop or two somewhere after they leave the workplace. They, most of them married, are going out only to be seen, while the predators are going out to find a companion for the night. Some of these not so young guys have several things in common. They are either retired, divorced, or widowed, and they all still enjoy the company of a lovely woman. If that woman happens to be nice-looking and rich, it's just icing on the cake. They may not be the all-night-long rooster they used to be, but with modern medicine, they can still get the job done.

The cougars are going out to find a younger man with a lot of stamina, maybe just for tonight, maybe the whole weekend, or maybe for a short-term relationship. The stamina part is not only sex but also partying and dancing. If they have to pay a little bit along the way, so be it. They consider it a cost of doing business. The rewards usually outweigh the cost.

Around 5 p.m., Terry Graff strides into Patio's, a lovely, lively outdoor restaurant and bar located on the waterfront in Little River. Their huge deck, which has several different levels, is built around beautiful old live oak trees. The view is spectacular as the patrons watch boat traffic on the waterway from their shaded vista. Terry is 52 years old and a retired IRS regional supervisor. He is 5'7", 170 pounds with a receding hairline. He wears wire-rim glasses and seems to have a rather outgoing, happy-go-lucky personality. The ladies say he reminds them of George on *Seinfeld*. They think of him as a cuddly teddy bear. It is happy hour at Patio's and the place is starting to fill up. A two-piece band is playing oldies but goodies and throwing in a little country on the side. Several lovely, mature women at the bar wave at Terry and invite him over for a drink. He has a big grin on his face as he meanders over to where the women are sitting. He thinks to himself, *it's going to be a good night.*

ॐॐ

Seymour Groves walks around to the side outdoor deck entrance of Filet's. The restaurant is located next to the waterway and the Little River Swing Bridge in North Myrtle Beach. They accommodate inside seating as well as outdoor seating on the deck. The deck area, referred to as Capt'n Dilligaf's Tiki Bar, overlooks the Harbourgate Marina and the waterway. It has a nice-sized bar, which is where most of the action takes place. If a predator or cougar is looking for some action, they hang out on the deck or sit at the bar. If they are just there for dinner and to listen to the music, which is provided every night during the tourist season and on weekends the rest of the year, they find themselves a table. Table cougars are usually off limits, unless they are new to the Tiki Bar area, and bar cougars are fair game. The same goes for the predators. Seymour is 58 years old and a retired U.S. Postal Service manager. He is 5'11", 180 pounds with a full head of dark black hair. He wears black-rimmed glasses which match his hair. He seems to be very quiet and reserved, sort of reminds one of Roy Orbison. The women are intrigued with him. Seymour takes a seat at the bar. Let the good times begin.

ॐॐ

Norman Burmeister decides to checkout Cozy O's tonight. It is a small Italian bistro next to The Food Lion in Little River. He has heard through the grapevine that the action there is light but very quality controlled. In other words, the women are discreet and wealthy. Norman is 57 years old and a retired Air Force dentist. He is 6' tall, 185 pounds with thinning brown hair, a square jaw, and dark, thick eyebrows. He wears contact lenses and he has a rather contemptuous personality. He acts and looks more like a college professor than an Air Force dentist. The women are inquisitive about him. He figures he will fit in well with this crowd. He arrives about 6:30, finds a place at the bar and checks out the population. The livestock looks good. There is a three-piece band playing jazz and he feels very comfortable right away. He could score big tonight.

ৰ্জ্ঞ

Around 7:00 in the evening, Larry Meggart walks into Mulligan's Irish Pub in Little River. Mulligan's is located next to the Cypress Bay golf course, so the views from the restaurant are awe-inspiring. Larry is 59 years old and a retired Secret Service agent. He is 6'1", 200 pounds with a short military haircut. His eyes are 20-20. He has an uppity introverted personality. He could be a double for Clint Eastwood. The women flock to him. He takes a seat in the bar area with his back to the wall. He has not been in here for a while but the last time he was, he scored big time. He likes to move from location to location so as not to look too familiar to people. He enjoys keeping a low profile. A lovely middle-aged woman walks into the bar area and sits across from him. Looks like it could be home run time again.

All four of these men have dated Ellen Thorn. Three of them had good results and one of them, the hunter, got nowhere fast.

Chapter 14: Hitting the Streets

The last time I spoke with Detective Concile, she was not getting answers from anyone about her two missing persons, Ellen and Jack. I figure it's about time I go barhopping and see what information I can gather. Cathy and Beverly each volunteer to go with me but I think I will learn more on my own. Besides that, I don't want Beverly karate-chopping some old lady who makes a pass at me. Cathy tells me to go to either Martini's or Filet's and not to wait too late because older people go to bed early, that way they can get up and be home by 11:00. She laughs so I guess she is just pulling my leg.

I walk into Martini's around 7:30 and the young, attractive hostess asks me if I would like a table and would anyone be joining me. I tell her no thanks, unless she is available for dinner later. She lowers her head, hiding her smile, as a pale flush lights her neck and brightens her cheeks. Before she can answer, I tell her I am just kidding and that I am just going to the bar for a drink. Then as I am walking away she says, "If I can be of any service later, please let me know. I get off at ten."

I raise my hand, wave, and walk into the bar area. I think to myself, *Mickke D, you've still got it*. I also remind myself this is business, not pleasure. I go to the far end of the bar and pick a location where I can see everything that's going on, who comes in, who goes out, and who is with whom. I order a Heineken with a frosted mug from a pleasant-speaking, nice-looking lady bartender who tells me her name is Kitty. I think she is also giving me the eye. I take a long drink of my beer and think maybe Cathy was right; maybe I had waited too long because the bar is not very busy.

After about thirty minutes, things begin to pick up. More folks wander into the bar area and begin making friends with whoever will talk to them. I'm thinking about a bathroom break so I tell Kitty to get me another beer and that I'll be right back. So far, it looks like she may be my best bet for information. Before heading off to the men's room, I ask her if she knows a woman named Ellen Thorn. She tells me she just started today and that she doesn't know anyone but me. I was right, she was giving me the eye. I grin and make my way to the restroom. As I'm passing an area where several small tables are set up, a woman in a wheelchair backs down in front of me and blocks my path.

"Hey sailor, buy a girl a drink?"

"Why yes ma'am, it would be my pleasure."

"Hey, deep six the ma'am crap. My name is Lexi Weakland. Who are you?"

"I'm Mickke D, my bar stool or your table?"

She winks. "Well, Mickke D, as you can see, I don't fit well at a bar so let's go to my place."

I follow her over to one of the small tables and she fits her chair up against it. I take a chair directly across from her. She is an attractive woman, I'm guessing in her early to mid-fifties, nicely dressed with strawberry blond hair. There's not a hair out of place, her make-up is light and perfect; and it looks as if she has just had her nails done.

I have my hand lying on the table. She puts her hand on mine and says in a mischievous tone of voice, "Before we get too serious, I want you to know something. Just because I'm in a wheelchair doesn't mean you and I can't get together for a drink later on sometime, once we get to know each other."

I place my other hand on top of hers and reply, "Well Lexi, before we get too serious, I would like to ask you a few questions. Is that going to hinder our relationship?"

She removes her hand from between mine as the bartender brings my beer over and takes a vodka tonic order from Lexi. "I guess that depends on the questions. I'm not into anything kinky. What do you want to know?"

"Well, how about this one. Do you know Ellen Thorn?"

"Whoa sailor, are you a cop? Am I wasting my valuable time on a cop?"

I try to reassure her. "No, I'm not a cop. I'm a private investigator. I'm a lot of things, but I am not a cop. I was hired by a friend of Ellen's to try and find out what happened to her."

She seems relieved. "Well, okay, sure I know Ellen. Everyone in North Myrtle Beach knows Ellen. What do you want to know about her?"

"So what do you think happened to her?"

"I don't know, but if I were you I would be looking into her latest boyfriend, a guy named Jack Miller."

"Therein lies the problem Lexi, Mr. Miller is missing also. Did you know him?"

"Yea, I knew him. He is a sleazebag. You find him and you'll probably find Ellen."

I decide to question her statement. "So if he was such a sleazebag, what did Ellen see in him?"

She rolls her eyes. "From what I understand, Ellen lived a lot of years without some of the finer physical things in life, if you know what I mean? So when her husband died, she came down here and was trying to make up for lost time."

"So you're saying she had multiple intimate friends?"

"Well, not necessarily multiple, but when she found quality and quantity in a partner, she could overlook personality discrepancies. Jack had quite a few of those."

"So who were some of her other partners, let's say within the past year, if you don't mind me asking?"

She takes a sip of the drink the bartender had set down. "Well, I don't know Mickke D, what's in it for me?"

Before I answer that question, I am thinking to myself, I can't remember the last time I actually turned down sex. Why am I thinking about turning it down this time. Am I that wrapped up in Beverly and if I am, why? She is not who she claims to be and the last thing I need is another ex-wife. In addition, I have never let business get in the way of pleasure before.

Lexi breaks the uncomfortable silence. "Earth to Mickke D, are you in there?"

I stop daydreaming. "Lexi Weakland, I'm going to be very honest with you. I'm in sort of a relationship currently, so I'll have to take a rain check on any new relationships right now." I can't believe I actually said that.

"Why are all the good ones always taken?" she sighs as her bottom lip puckers. "Well, are you going to write these names down or do you have a photographic memory?"

I get a small notepad and pen from my corduroy jacket pocket. "Okay, sock it to me Lexi Weakland, I'm ready."

"I'll just bet you are but I'll give you the names anyway. I know of four guys she has dated in the past year, other than Jack; Seymour Groves, Terry Graff, Larry Meggart, and Norman Burmiester."

I continue my information gathering. "Did she have any problems with any of them or with anyone else? Did anyone ever threaten her?"

"Not that I know of, but we don't usually give out negative information about any of our partners. That would show we had made a mistake in judgment and no one wants to admit that. Just let the next girl find out for herself. You know what they say, what's one person's junk is another person's treasure. Some women like kinky guys and others don't. Personally, I don't."

"So what you're saying is some of these guys were kinky?" I bluntly ask.

"No, I didn't say that but you can draw your own conclusions."

I offer to buy her another drink but she says she is good. She writes her phone number on a cocktail napkin and tells me to call her when my present friend dumps me. I tell her she's number one on my list when that happens. After my bathroom break and as I am leaving, the bartender and hostess both wave goodbye and tell me to come back real soon. I'm not sure where I'll put them on my list.

The names Lexi Weakland gave me are the same as the ones Cathy gave me. She also would not admit to Ellen having any problems with her male friends. It sounds like Sam was right. The cougars are a discreet society and information is not readily forthcoming. I guess I'll put these four guys on my suspect list and go from there.

Chapter 15: Connie Smith at the Beach

Connie Smith arrives at the Myrtle Beach International Airport at 4 p.m. on the Saturday flight from Grand Cayman. She was a little concerned about leaving Grand Cayman and returning to the States for the first time. She had the feeling everyone was watching her and that the customs official was going to pull her out of line and arrest her. She encountered no problems, even though she was using her own passport and photo. Maybe her old boss, Senator Brazile, has accepted the fact that the money he lost did not really belong to him and she is free to come and go as she pleases.

She is very nervous and constantly looking around as she waits to retrieve her luggage. Once she has her luggage, she goes into the women's restroom and puts on her disguise. She goes in as Connie Smith, former private secretary to United States Senator R. Gene Brazile and comes out as Paula German, schoolteacher from Cleveland, Ohio. She had a fake driver's license made while on Grand Cayman and she slips it in front of her real license in her wallet. She had business cards produced with her as a tutor, her new name, and a fake address in Cleveland. She plans to pay for everything in cash.

She rents a car and checks into the Avista Resort in North Myrtle Beach. She pays for three nights, up front. She tells the Avista clerk the same thing she told the rental car attendant, someone stole her credit card wallet in the airport and cash is all she has for now. They both accept the cash.

As far as her itinerary is concerned, she did some checking online and discovered the shag craze in North Myrtle Beach. She plans to check it out tonight after a walk on the beach and dinner. She read online about Brookgreen Gardens so she picks up a brochure in the resort lobby and plans a day trip there on Tuesday before her 7 p.m. flight back to the Caymans. Sunday is going to be a beach day and she plans to shop on Monday as well as look at some beachfront condos. Online, she found two independent real estate offices in North Myrtle Beach, Mickke D Real Estate and Beach & Country Realty. She feels as if she should invest a portion of her money but maybe not on Grand Cayman. It would be great to have a second home in the states.

Paula decides to pass on the beach walk. She goes to the front desk to ask for directions to a nice restaurant that isn't too far away and they suggest she try Filet's down by the swing bridge. It's close and should be easy to find. She locates the restaurant and takes a seat at a table out on the deck so she can watch the boats traverse the waterway. The moment she sits down, she feels eyes peering her way. She turns and looks toward the bar area and several men all wave at her at the same time. At first, she begins to panic. She thinks they may know her but since she is in disguise, she quickly decides they are just horny old men.

Her waitress appears, introduces herself as Carol Anne, and Paula orders a glass of Cabernet Sauvignon. She asks Carol Anne, "Why are those men staring at me?"

The waitress turns toward the men and motions for them to turn around. "Don't worry, they are just old guys who take Viagra and want to show off. They think they're twenty-five again but they're harmless and besides that they usually go after the older more mature women, not a beautiful young woman like yourself."

Paula puts that comment in her memory bank for recall when it comes to tip time. She puts in her order, relaxes, and watches the waterway traffic go by and even gets to see the swing bridge open and close. She is finally relaxing and enjoying herself. Her dinner arrives, prime-rib medium rare, garlic mashed potatoes, and a vegetable medley. Everything is delicious. She finishes her dinner and orders a cup of decaffeinated coffee. She takes a sip of her coffee, looks up, and there is a man standing next to her table staring at her. He has dark black hair and he is wearing large, black-rimmed glasses.

He says to her, "Sweetheart, we could be identical twins. Are you into incest?"

The comment catches her by surprise. She is momentarily amazed, appalled, repelled, and fascinated by his indignation. She had forgotten that she also had coal black hair and black rimmed glasses. "Look pervert, I'm not interested, go back up to the bar and play with yourself, just leave me alone."

"Sorry missy, that was supposed to be a joke. I guess you don't have a sense of humor. I won't bother you anymore."

The stranger turns abruptly and goes back to the bar area where he begins a conversation with an older, rich-looking woman. He slowly melts away into the crowd and Paula can no longer see him.

She wonders if she was too harsh or too mean to the man. He may have been a nice person. Oh well, she did not come here to have an affair or overnight fling. She finishes her coffee, pays her check, leaves Carol Anne a nice tip, and walks out the side entrance heading toward the parking lot.

Norman Burmeister is on his way into Filet's. He is walking toward her. He stops. "Don't I know you from somewhere, maybe the Academy Awards?"

She stops, looks him right in the eyes, and says, "No you don't know me and I'm not interested." She continues walking.

Norman calls out, "Have a nice evening."

She doesn't turn around, just waves her hand. Wow, this is the most action she has had in a long time. She smiles and thinks, "it wouldn't take much for a girl to get laid in this town."

Chapter 16: Jim

I get to the office around 10 Monday morning, which is about my normal time to make an appearance. On the days Beverly works, she comes in at 9 and Mark's wife Jannie works the days that Beverly is off. Jim and Mark come in at various times depending on the work that needs done. I no more than walk in the front door when Beverly tells me Jim needs to see me right away.

I walk into his office and he motions for me to close the door. Maybe he is feeling a little bit antsy about Beverly also. I hope this is not more bad news about her.

"You are not going to believe the call I got this morning," he excitedly says to me. "I have people at the airport keeping an eye out for any Connie Smith's that are flying somewhere. They can put a name into their computer and are able to check all flights from anywhere in the states. Well, anyway, my contact calls me and says a Connie Smith flew into Myrtle Beach on Saturday from Grand Cayman."

"Wow, that is good news. Did you call the senator?"

"No, not yet. It gets better. I then checked with another contact from a car rental company. There is no record of any Connie Smith renting a car on Saturday and better yet, there is no record of anyone by that name checking into a condo or hotel along the Grand Strand on Saturday."

I ask him with a puzzled look on my face, "How are you able to find out all of this?"

He grins. "You really don't want to know. Just remember this conversation when you get that occasional receipt for a golf foursome on my expense account."

I ask, "So, do you think someone met her at the airport and took her to a private residence or condo?"

Jim shakes his head. "I don't know, it's as if she just disappeared after arriving here. I have a call out for any possible credit card purchases but that has come up empty also."

"I'm glad you didn't call the senator because we really have nothing to tell him. She may not even be his Connie Smith and even if she is, we have no idea where she is staying. Let me know if you find her. By the way, does she have a round trip fare and if so, when is she going back?"

Again, he grins and says, "I already thought about that. She has a flight back to the Caymans Tuesday at 7 p.m. I'll be there to see if she shows up. If she does, hopefully I'll be able to determine if she is the one we're looking for. The senator sent me a photo."

Chapter 17: Connie/Paula

Paula gets into her rental car and leaves Filet's. She drives down Sea Mountain Highway on her way to Main Street, which is just around the corner from where she is staying. It's time to check out this shag thing.

While on Sea Mountain Highway, she looks for and locates Mickke D Real Estate and Beach & Country Realty. They are almost side-by-side. She may just flip a coin to see which one she will call, although she does like the name Mickke D.

She goes into Fat Harold's Beach Club first and spends about an hour watching people do the official dance of South Carolina, the shag. The shag is a lively partner dance done primarily to beach music. The term "Carolina shag" is thought to have originated along the coast between Myrtle Beach and Wilmington during the 1940s. North Myrtle Beach has always claimed it is the "Shag Capital" of the South.

While at Fat Harold's, she is hit on by several guys, including Terry Graff and Larry Meggart, who actually seem upset that she refuses their invitation. She then goes down the street to the OD Arcade and spends another forty-five minutes there. She has a glass of wine in each place and really enjoys herself. While she is at ODs, several men ask her to dance, and offer to buy her drinks, but she declines their invitation. She checks her watch and it's almost 11:30. She is starting to fade quickly, so it's time to go back and get a good night's sleep.

She crosses Main Street to get to the public parking lot next to Fat Harold's and looks for her car. There is a major problem once she locates it. The left rear tire is flatter than a pancake. She curses under her breath, puts her hands on her hips and says aloud, "Great, now what do I do?"

She hears a door open and looks in the direction of the sound. There is a pick-up truck parked in front of her car and the driver's door opens. A man steps out. He is bald, middle-aged, and decent looking. He's wearing a hip-length brown leather jacket and for some strange reason, sunglasses. She wonders about the leather jacket, it's not that cold but he looks good in it.

"Excuse me, but it looks like you have a problem." He says, although he is difficult to understand. She thinks he must have gum or something in his mouth.

This stranger seems nice enough, so she asks, "Do you by chance know how to change a tire?"

He walks over and stands beside her. He looks at the tire and then looks her directly in the eyes, and says in a garbled, deep tone of voice, "Yes I can, but that tire is not your only problem."

His voice almost sounds familiar. She looks back at him with a bewildered look on her face. "Really, what other problem do I have?"

The hunter pulls his hunting knife from his pocket and places it at her throat while putting his other hand over her mouth so she can't scream. Fear strikes her face like a wave of fire. The knife he is holding is the same one he used to slash her tire. He pushes her over toward his pick-up truck, opens the passenger door and pushes her into the passenger seat, which is covered by a clear plastic drop cloth. Before she has time to react, he takes the knife away from her throat and pushes it deep into her abdomen while turning the blade. He clings to the anger coursing through him. He wants her to suffer.

His eyes light up with excitement. He whispers into her ear, "You're a bitch, just like my dead ex-wife."

Blood vessels and arteries are severed, organs are ruptured. She gasps and her eyes get as big as saucers as she feels her life slowly fading away, then her world dissolves into a black, somber darkness.

The hunter looks around and sees no one. He buckles the seatbelt around her, gets into the pick-up and drives west on Route

9. He drives slowly into the same swamp where he disposed of Ellen and Jack. Once he is sure there is nobody there, he pulls down to the edge of the water, retrieves the johnboat he has hidden in the bushes, wraps her body in a tarp, and with the help of some cinder blocks and rope, he disposes of Connie Smith's body. Billybob Swamp has just claimed another victim of the hunter.

The hunter returns the johnboat to where he had it hidden and he returns to the beach. He had a great time tonight, he saw her, her met her, he was rejected by her, and so he killed her.

Chapter 18: Another Missing Person

The following Tuesday around noon, the condo cleaning service knocks on the door of Paula German's condo at Avista. No one answers. The cleaning person unlocks the door and finds Paula's belongings still there. Checkout time is 11:00. She calls the front desk and is told to finish her other condos and then go back to Paula's condo. Around 2 p.m., she returns and nothing has changed. The front desk tells her not to worry about the condo, the complex has plenty of empty condos available. Maybe the occupant just got her checkout day mixed up.

∽⸺

 Tuesday evening about 5 p.m., Jim arrives at the Myrtle Beach Airport with a photo of Connie Smith in hand. He looks around and says hello to several of the airport police, who he knows. He shows them Connie's picture and asks them to keep an eye out for her. He tells them she is not dangerous or a threat in any way, but if they see her, please let him know.

 At around 6 p.m. he sits down across from the airline that Connie is using to fly back to Grand Cayman. He brought along a golf magazine to read while waiting. He watches but sees no one matching her description check in. When he hears the airline attendant make the final boarding call for Connie's flight to Grand Cayman, he decides it's time to ask some questions.

 Jim flags down one of his airport police buddies and goes up to the counter. He asks if Connie Smith has checked in for her flight back to Grand Cayman. The policeman vouches for him and the attendant checks her passenger list. "I'm sorry, Connie Smith has not checked in."

Jim is confused. He watches as the flight for Grand Cayman leaves without Connie Smith.

❧❦

Wednesday morning, Jim comes directly to my office as soon as he arrives at work. "She never showed up, she was not on the flight back to the Caymans."

I look bewildered. "What are you saying? We have another missing person?"

"I don't know. Maybe she came here to disappear, maybe that was her plan, maybe she decided to stay," Jim says.

"Okay, let me call Detective Concile and see if she has had any calls about a new missing person recently."

I place the call and Sam tells me she has not received any calls about a missing person. She asks, "Would this person be another friend of Ellen Thorn or Jack Miller?"

"No detective, this would pertain to a completely different case," I reply.

"Mickke D, how come every time you get involved in something, bodies begin to pile up?"

"I don't know Sam, but if you get a new missing person call, please let me know." I hang up before she can scold me for calling her Sam and not Detective Concile.

❧❦

Wednesday afternoon a call from the Avista Resort is transferred to Detective Concile. The assistant manager at the resort thinks that one of his guests may be a missing person. Sam does some checking and discovers a rental car had been towed to the impound lot from a public lot on Main Street in North Myrtle Beach next to Fat Harolds Sunday night. The name the rental company gave them was Paula German. Sam just shakes her head and thinks, *Mickke D, you bastard.*

Chapter 19: Where's Paula?

Sam opens her cell phone but hesitates pushing the buttons to call Mickke D. The pause doesn't last long. She takes a deep breath and dials the number.

"This is Mickke D, how can I help you?"

Once again, she pauses, but finally says, "This is Detective Concile. It seems as if you may have been right. We had a call for a missing person at the Avista Resort in North Myrtle Beach. A woman named Paula German left for dinner on Saturday night and has not been seen or heard from since. We towed a rental car with a flat tire from a public parking lot next to Fat Harolds Sunday night and the rental company said it had been rented to a Paula German."

I decide to jab the needle in a little bit and reply, "I appreciate you calling me, detective. I know it isn't easy for you to admit I might have been correct."

"Whatever. I'm not admitting anything. I'm just trying to find some missing persons."

I jab again. "Sorry detective, I'm just in a playful mood today."

"Yeah, right." She responds.

"Say detective, did the resort give you a description of Paula German?"

I hear her shuffling papers on her desk. "Yes, they said she was in her late forties to early fifties, medium height and weight, dark black hair and large black-rimmed glasses, a very striking and attractive woman. They stated she looked a lot like Cher with a few added pounds."

I think for a minute. "Did they know where she was going for dinner?"

"Well, maybe. The front desk suggested Filet's to her."

"So are you going to send someone to talk to Fat Harold's and Filet's?"

Now she jabs the needle in a little bit while smiling to herself. "No, I'm not. There's no body. The car was clean. She could be shacked up with some guy for all I know. My hands are tied until a relative files a missing persons report or a body is discovered. Why don't you go talk to Fat Harold's and Filet's? You're the private eye. But whatever you do, don't shoot anyone, blow up their building, burn it down, or piss someone off."

I think to myself, *touché.* "Let me see what I can find out and before you say it, yes I will keep you advised and in the loop."

As soon as I hang up, I look out the window and Jim's car is in the parking lot. I'm surprised because it's such a nice day, I figured he would be on the golf course today. I go to his office and tell him about my conversation with Sam and he says everything matches Connie Smith's description except the black hair and black glasses. I ask him if he has a photo of Connie Smith. I remember him telling me the senator sent him a photo of Connie. He opens a file folder and produces the photo for me. I gaze at the photo and say to Jim, "She is an attractive woman. Do you mind? I need to borrow this for a day or two."

"No problem. I'll leave the file folder right here on my desk."

I take the photo and return to my office. I call a friend of mine who draws caricatures at the Myrtle Beach Mall, Calvin Peat. Calvin is a local artist and a super nice guy.

"Calvin, Mickke D here. Are you at the mall today? I need a photo touched up."

He laughs. "No, I'm over at Tanger today, right outside the food court. You mean you're not going to use your high school graduation picture on your real estate card anymore?"

"Very funny. I'll see you in about thirty minutes."

Before leaving the office, I ask Jim if he wants to ride along but he tells me if he's lucky, he thinks he can get nine holes in before dark.

I arrive at Tanger thirty minutes later and find Calvin. I show him the photo. "Calvin, my man, I need you to give this lovely lady long black hair and bangs like Cher, and also fairly large black-rimmed glasses. Do you think you can do that?"

He laughs. "Are you kidding me? No problem, a piece of cake, just watch the master and be amazed."

He was right. In five minutes, Connie Smith becomes Paula German. At least that's what I think. I now need to take the photo to Avista, Filet's, and Fat Harold's to see if they recognize her.

֍֍

On the way back from Tanger, I stop at the Avista Resort. I go up to a lovely young, red-haired vixen at the front desk and before I can flash my PI card she says, "Hi, I'm Heather, how can I help y'all? Are y'all checkin' in?"

Her sexy southern accent catches me off guard. I regain my composure and tell her I am looking into the disappearance of Paula German. Heather frowns. "Oh, darn, I was hoping you would be staying with us for a while."

She makes a call and within seconds, a man appears from around the corner. He introduces himself as Martin Mitchell and he was on duty the night that Paula German disappeared.

"Are you with the police?" he asks sarcastically.

I hand him my business card and say, "No, I'm a private investigator looking into the case. The police can't do much unless a body is discovered. May I show you a photo?"

His demeanor softens. "Of course, we will help in any way we can. My only concern is we do not want any bad publicity for our resort."

"No problem, we just want to find this lady." I show him the photo.

With no hesitation he says, "Oh, that's her. No doubt about it."

I thank Heather and Mr. Mitchell for their time. Heather winks and gives me one of her cards. I wink back, give her one of my cards and return to my vehicle, shaking my head. Female encounters like this never happened to me before I was dating Beverly. I guess it's either feast or famine.

ॐॐ

The time is about 4:00 and I figure this may be a good time to stop by Filet's before the evening dinner rush. I show my PI card and ask for the manager. He appears shortly and introduces himself as Ian Howard. "How may I help you Mr. MacCandlish? Is this about that missing lady Ellen Thorn and Jack Miller? The police, right after their disappearance, questioned me along with several of my staff. I'm afraid we were not much help."

"No, this is about another possible missing woman. Her name is Paula German and we think she may have had dinner here last Saturday night. Would any of your waitresses from last Saturday night happen to be here tonight?"

"Let me check my roster from that night. I'll be right back."

He returns post haste with a smile on his face. "Yes, Carol Anne was here last Saturday night. Let me get her for you."

He returns in a few minutes with Carol Anne, a bouncy, very Italian, middle-aged woman. I show her the photo and she immediately replies, "Oh sure, I remember her. Seemed like a nice lady. Why do you want to know about her?"

I reply, "There's a possibility she may be a missing person. Do you remember what time she left here Saturday night and if she left with anyone?"

"Sure. Ian, can you check my receipts for last Saturday night? She was at table six. She had prime rib and a glass of Cabernet Sauvignon."

Mr. Howard and I both look at each other in disbelief.

She gets the drift from our expressions. "Oh, some people just make an impression on me. She was one of those people."

Ian leaves and quickly returns with a slip of paper. "The bill was printed at 8:46 and she paid with cash."

I ask, "So Carol Anne, what time do you think she left?"

"Well, I would say pretty close to 9:30. She stayed for awhile, had some coffee and listened to the music."

As long as she is answering, I'm asking. "Did she leave with anyone?"

"Oh no, a couple of guys hit on her, but she was not interested. I think I even saw a guy hit on her as she was leaving, but she just kept on walking. I thought she was cool. I hope she's all right."

"Do you remember who any of the guys were?"

"No, not by name, but I would know them if I saw them again."

I give Carol Anne my card and ask her to call me if she remembers anything else about that evening that may be helpful. I thank them for their time and leave the restaurant. I'm going to put Filet's on my eating list. Looks like a great place to bring Beverly for dinner.

Since I'm two for two, I decide to stop by Fat Harold's Beach Club before going back to the office.

Fat Harold's is one of the oldest shag destinations in North Myrtle Beach. It was established in 1959 and has been at its current location on Main Street since 1992. It has several large dance floors where DJs spin 60s classic beach music and people of all ages shag dance. The patrons enjoy feel-good fun and enthusiasm for the music, and the dance style is very infectious.

Although I am not a dancer, Beverly talked me into going there one evening and she had a great time. She tried to explain to me that the shag consists of six counts, which are the key to doing it correctly. She said what makes it unique is how you move your body and feet within the basic count. I just shook my head in agreement, wondering to myself, "where does she get this information." She danced with several guys while I just watched and continued to tell her I had two left feet. She made it very clear to me that they gave free dance lessons; however, it seems as if I was always busy or had some sort of an excuse on those occasions.

I go into Fat Harold's, flash my PI card, and ask for the person in charge. A call is made and Miss LuLu comes over to me, introduces herself as the office manager, and asks how she can help me. I give her my card and show her the picture of Connie Smith, aka Paula German. I ask her if she remembers her from last Saturday night. She tells me she was there last Saturday night along with maybe a hundred other women. She rather looked familiar, but she could not be sure. I thank her for her time and head back to the office. Well, two out of three ain't bad. I'm convinced in my mind that Paula and Connie are one in the same.

I'm going to have Jim call the senator and give him an update. It seems our two cases may be entwined.

Chapter 20: The Senator

North Carolina Senator Brazile had asked Jim not to send any information about Connie by e-mail or fax. Jim calls the senator on his private line. "Senator, its Jim Bolin with GSI in North Myrtle Beach. Do you have a minute for an update?"

"Yes, Mr. Bolin, do you have any good news for me?"

"Well, senator, yes and no. We think Connie Smith actually made a trip to Myrtle Beach from the Grand Caymans but we cannot confirm that she made the return trip back. The resort where she was staying actually called the police and listed her as a missing person."

"Very interesting, Mr. Bolin. Was she using her real name?"

"Again, yes and no. She flew here using her real name but changed it to Paula German once she arrived in Myrtle Beach."

The senator hesitates for a second. "Do you think she is still alive, Mr. Bolin?"

"Hard to say, senator. We have several missing persons we're looking into right now and there is the possibility a serial killer is on the loose down here."

"Thank you, Mr. Bolin. Send me a statement for your services and if you hear anything else, please let me know."

"No problem, but don't you want us to check into the Grand Cayman connection for you?"

"No, not at this time. If I change my mind, I'll let you know." The conversation ends.

Damn, Jim is thinking to himself. *I could use a trip to Grand Cayman. I've heard there are some great golf courses there.*

After hanging up, Senator Brazile leans back in his large, over-stuffed desk chair, puts his feet up, and lights a cigar. After blowing a bluish grey circle with the smoke, he smiles and quietly says to no one, "Got ya, Connie."

He now believes Connie is no longer a threat and possibly dead. Now he just has to figure out how he can get his money back. He really doesn't want to get GSI involved any deeper in this. He knows some people in the banking business in the Caymans. He will make some calls and pull in some favors.

Chapter 21: Larry Meggart

The following morning, I decide I should probably see my suspects up close and personal. I call Jim into my office. It's raining, so he can't play golf.

"Jim, I'd like you to call some of your restaurant and night-club friends and send them a description of our suspects in these missing person cases. See if they will contact you if they see any of them in their businesses."

"Sure, but why do you want me to do that?"

"I'd like to meet these guys in a neutral environment and see if I can learn anything about them."

ᔧ᷈᷍ᔨ

Two days later around 8:00 in the evening, my phone rings. It's Jim. He tells me he just got a call from one of his contacts at The Night Fever Club in Myrtle Beach. One of our suspects just walked into the club.

I change my clothes, pick Jim up and we go down to the club. We arrive around 9:00. Jim tells me on the way down that usually the club doesn't start hopping until about 10:00. I just stare at him and don't ask how he knows this.

Once inside, Jim introduces me to Sharon Coyote, who is one of the owners and Jim's contact. Sharon is a very attractive blonde in her mid-thirties. She introduces me to her husband Scott who is the DJ. Both of them seem to know Jim very well. Again, I do not ask.

From the description Cathy and Lexi gave me, I spot Larry Meggart sitting at the corner of the bar drinking a beer. He is in a conversation with the bartender who looks as if she is young enough to be his granddaughter. I stand at the bar on Larry's right and Jim takes a seat directly across from him at the bar.

Night Fever has a beautiful decorative bar with a large dance floor, which at this early time of night was not being used. Once my eyes adjust to the darkness, I decide to familiarize myself with the surroundings. As I look around, I see two pool tables in the middle section behind and to the left of Larry and behind him a sunken great room area with lounge chairs and small tables. Quite nice and rather up-scale. Scott is playing some disco music and mixing in some jazz along the way. There are probably twenty people in the bar, a nice, small, seemingly friendly crowd.

Larry glances our way and then picks up his beer. He goes over to one of the unoccupied pool tables before I have a chance to start a conversation with him. I leave Jim at the bar and go over to the pool table where Larry is chalking his cue stick. I ask him if he would like to play a little nine ball for a beer. He accepts the challenge and I rack. He breaks and the match is on.

He introduces himself. "I'm Larry, I don't think I've seen you in here before."

"I'm Mickke D, nice to meet you Larry," shaking his hand, which is firm and somewhat aggressive. "First time for me, what about you?"

"Look Mickke D, cut the bull shit. What do you want? This is not my first rodeo. Is the other guy at the bar your back up? Are you the police or just a fool?"

He catches me off guard. "No, I'm not the police, I'm a local PI. Do you mind if I ask you a few questions?"

He replies, "Not only am I not going to answer any questions, I'm going to plant this cue stick on the side of your head if you don't just turn around and walk away."

I notice out the front window there are buses unloading partygoers from a local resort. This is not the time to start a ruckus.

Since he seems very serious, I lay my cue on the table, raise my hands and say, "Sorry man, no problem. Sorry I bothered you." I turn and walk away.

I go back to where I left Jim. He is talking golf with two lovely ladies. They watch as my face turns from a very serious look into a stern glare. They get up and move down to the end of the bar.

"Did you learn anything?" Jim asks.

I give him a blank look and reply, "Yeah, that went real well. The only thing I learned was that he is either ex-military or Fed and that he is not a happy camper. He spotted us the minute we walked in the door."

"Do you want me to talk to him? Maybe I can determine if he's ex-FBI."

For a second, I think about saying yes, but this is too nice a place for a fight to begin. And of course, I know I will be paying the bill.

"No, finish your beer and let's hit the road. That is unless you want me to leave and those two lovely girls can give you a ride home."

Jim grins, "I don't think so. I have a 7:30 tee time in the morning. I'll save them for a rainy day."

If I had had that much self-control, I may still be married to one of my ex-wives. On the way out, I notice he slips both girls his business card. On the ride home, I ask him to check with his friends at the Bureau and see what he can find out about Larry Meggart and my other suspects. I have just moved Mr. Meggart to the top of my suspect list.

Chapter 22: The Call

It's Saturday night and I'm grilling a steak out on the deck when my cell phone rings. My dog Blue is hoping I make a mistake and drop it on the deck. His ears perk up when he hears the phone ring and he peers at both deck entrances, looking for intruders. The sound of the phone stirs feelings deep inside my gut which I have been trying to dismiss. My deck has been the scene of some rather bizarre happenings in recent times and one of them began with a phone call.

It has been several days since I interviewed potential witnesses from Filet's, Avista, and Fat Harold's. The caller is Carol Anne, the waitress I spoke with at Filet's. She tells me that one of the men who hit on Paula German is at the bar on the outside deck. I thank her and tell her I am on my way.

I look at the half-cooked steak on the grill and then at Blue. He is sitting at attention next to the grill. His eyes are wide open, ears are up, tail is wagging, and saliva is dripping from his mouth. He raises his left paw for a high five. What a pathetic looking dog. I cut off a hunk of steak and put Blue inside the screened-in porch with his treat. The remainder of the steak goes into the fridge, to be consumed by me later.

ॐॐ

I arrive at Filet's, walk around the outside of the building next to the waterway and enter the outside deck area. Carol Anne spots me and comes over.

She puts her hand up to her mouth and whispers, "That's the guy at the end of the bar, the one with the black hair and black-rimmed glasses. He's talking to the woman with the shoulder length gray hair. Her name is Page Rivers and I think his name is Seymour."

"Thanks Carol Anne, I appreciate you calling me."

She starts to leave and then comes back. "You're not going to believe it but the other guy who hit on her while she was leaving just showed up also. That's him standing outside talking to that lady with the blond hair."

"Do you know their names?" I ask.

"I don't know his name, but that's the guy. The blonde's name is Connie Clark, she's a regular here."

I'm beginning to think I should have called Jim to come with me. Instead of one suspect, I now have two, and one of them could be a cold-blooded serial killer. I opt to check out the guy with the black-rimmed glasses first, only because he was the first one Carol Anne pointed out to me.

I order a Heineken from the bartender and mosey on down to the end of the bar where Seymour is holding court. As I approach the area, Page turns around, looks me up and down and says, "Well, hello there. I don't think we've met. I'm Page and who are you?"

"I'm Mickke D. Nice to meet you Page."

"Cute name Mickke D, what brings you here tonight?"

"Well, since you asked, I'm looking for a woman named Ellen Thorn. Do you know her?"

Page looks irritated. "Haven't seen her in several weeks. Someone said she just up and left town. Someone else said she and her boyfriend Jack just up and ran away together. I don't really care. Is there anything I can do for you?"

"Allow me to clarify my last statement. What I met by 'looking for her' is that I'm a private investigator and I'm checking into her possible disappearance." I hand her my business card.

The semi-loud drone of banter quickly dies down to a gentle muffle of words as most of the patrons in the general area turn and look at me. This only lasts a few seconds and then the volume returns to its original level.

I notice Seymour glance at me with a scornful look on his face and then he inches closer to where Page and I are standing. He looks straight at her and says, "Page, are you ready for another drink?"

"Sure thing, sweetheart. Say hello to Mickke D. He's trying to find Ellen."

"Hey, Mickke D, I'm Seymour. I didn't know Ellen was missing."

"Well, her girlfriend thinks she is, so I'm just looking into the possibility that she may be a missing person. By the way, did you know Ellen?"

"Only by reputation. She was known as the Cougar Queen."

I decide to throw Seymour a high and tight fastball to see if he backs off the plate. "That's funny Seymour, several people have told me you dated her."

"Not that I can remember, but then again, I've slept since then."

Page chimes in, "Sure you did darling. I remember you telling me that."

Seymour looks befuddled but quickly responds. "Well, maybe. I guess she did not make a big impression on me."

Before I have a chance to ask another question, I notice Connie Clark tap Page on the shoulder and say, "Hey Page, who's your new friend?"

"Hey yourself, this is Mickke D. Mickke D, this is Connie Clark and Norman Burmeister," as she points to Carol Anne's unknown male.

Things are starting to get complicated to say the least. I now have two of my suspects almost side-by-side, Seymour Groves and Norman Burmeister. As I'm deciding who to ask what, Norman says, "Sure you did Seymour, I think we all dated Ellen at one time or another, although she was rather particular about whom she went out with, except for that guy Jack."

I think it's time for me to jump in. "So, did you guys know Jack well?'

Page answers quickly. "Yea, I knew him. He was a loser. I could never figure out what Ellen saw in him."

"Me neither," Connie says.

Looking at Seymour and Norman, I say, "What about you two guys. What did you think of Jack?"

Norman answers first. "I guess he was all right. I mainly saw him on the golf course. He played a decent game of golf."

Seymour has grown quiet. I look him directly in the eyes and ask, "What about you Seymour, did you know Jack?"

"Sorry, didn't know him that well. Guess I can't help you." Seymour takes Page's hand and they walk away. She turns back toward me, holds up my card, and waves.

I turn to continue my conversation with Connie and Norman but both of them have disappeared. It's as if I have a dome over me, the entire group has moved away. I'm standing there with a beer in my hand and no one to talk to. Cathy and Sam were right. The cougars and friends are a closed society.

After talking, though somewhat briefly to them, Seymour and Norman don't seem to fit the serial killer profile. Seymour is a little strange and somewhat possessive. Norman is rather stuck on himself but I doubt if either one of them could murder a person in cold blood. Larry Meggart is looking like my best suspect as of right now.

I finish my beer, find Carol Anne, and thank her for the call. It's time to get back to my half-grilled steak. As I am leaving, I feel the demons deep in my gut begin to tingle. I have the funny feeling someone is watching me. It's a trait I have that saved my ass several times while in the Army. My gaze rakes the deck area, searching for threats, while simultaneously looking for the two men who are on my short list of suspects. No one seems interested in me and no one is looking my way. Seymour and Norman have turned into ghosts. They are gone. As I leave, I am very alert and mindful of my surroundings. My demons settle down as I reach my SUV, but I still have that feeling that I'm being watched. I look around the parking lot before getting into my vehicle. Everything looks and seems quiet and peaceful.

Chapter 23: Night Fever

Page Rivers locates Connie Clark and they leave Filet's around 9:30 without Norman and Seymour. They decide to go to Night Fever in hopes of finding some dance partners. They arrive thirty minutes later and bump into Larry Meggart. He buys the girls a drink. All three of them end up on the dance floor and Larry is beginning to think this may end up as a three-way before the night is over.

Page and Connie have other ideas. They have two more drinks with Larry, several dances and then abruptly pick up their purses, thank him for the drinks, and start to leave the club. Larry is visibly upset. "Where are you going? We were just starting to get acquainted."

Page answers, "We have places to go and people to see."

He grabs her arm with a harsh grip and a begging stare. "Maybe I'll tag along."

She returns his stare with one of her own, but her stare is cold, not begging. "Let go of my arm. Maybe next time."

Larry releases his grip and says in a threatening tone, "Don't bet on it. I'm not the kind of guy who gives second chances."

"Well, I guess it's just our loss, isn't it?" Page and Connie go out the door and do not look back.

When they get to their car, Connie remarks, "What a jerk."

"You've got that right. Who does he think he is, God's gift to women?"

❧❧

The next and final stop Page and Connie make is Patio's in Little River where Connie left her car when she originally met Norman before heading off to Filet's. Page had started her evening there as well before heading off to Filet's with a couple of her girlfriends.

They arrive about 11:30 and both sit at the bar and order a cup of coffee. They both need to drive home, although neither one of them live far away. They no more than take their first sip when they both feel a hand on their shoulder. They turn and see Terry Graff with a big smile on his face. "Ladies, how are you doing tonight?"

Connie speaks first, "So far, without, and I am pretty sure it's going to end that way."

Page says, "What she just said, but you can buy us this coffee if you'd like."

Terry answers and never stops smiling. "I don't buy myself coffee. Why should I buy you ladies coffee? However, I will buy you a drink to spike those cups of coffee."

Page reaches back, pulls his hand from her shoulder and says, "I guess you don't understand English. We're not interested."

Terry's smile disappears. "Oh, I understand English, I just don't understand you two. Don't you ladies like men?"

Page is getting pissed. "Oh, we like men, we just don't like you. Now get lost."

Terry barks off a reply, "Feisty, aren't we? No problem, but someday you'll wish you had been nicer to me."

Connie replies, "Hopefully not in the near future."

The smirk on Terry's face broadens. His eyes sparkle with scorn. He turns and goes back to the group he had been talking with before Page and Connie arrived.

Connie finishes her coffee and says to Page, "Well Page, I've had enough fun for one night. I'm going home. I picked up a new mystery thriller from Wanda over at the Book Warehouse today. I think I'll take a good book to bed with me tonight."

Page replies with a sigh, "Me too, Connie, or maybe someone who has read a good book." They both laugh, "See you later. Be careful driving home." Then she adds, "Maybe one of us will get lucky and that Mickke D guy will be waiting for us."

"I wish. No problem, call me if you want to go out next weekend."

They leave Patio's, get into their cars, and drive away.

Chapter 24: Connie and Page

Connie Clark arrives safely at her condo on the waterway. She pulls into the one-car attached garage and closes the overhead door before she gets out of her car. She likes the idea that she doesn't have to get out into a dimly lit parking lot before entering her condo. She gets on the elevator and goes up to the fourth floor. She exits the elevator, walks down two doors, and puts her key in the lock. Just as she is turning the key, someone puts a hand on her shoulder. She jumps and turns around. She is relieved when she sees it is Martha from down the hall. "My God Martha, you scared the shit out of me. I almost pissed my panties."

"Hey girlfriend, you're coming in awfully late and you're alone. No overnight guest tonight?"

"No, just a few drinks and some dancing tonight. Did meet a cool guy at Filet's. He's a PI and his name is Mickke D."

"Cute name, does he look like Mike Hammer? I always thought he was hot."

"Well, maybe, except no mustache, no hat, and no cigarette."

Martha shrugs her shoulders. She turns and walks away while saying, "Oh well, can't have everything. Sorry I startled you. Catch you later."

Connie finishes unlocking her door, walks in and turns on the lights. She says to no one in particular, "Well, Page, Mickke D is not waiting for me. Maybe you'll get lucky."

She gets ready for bed, grabs her new book *Murder on the Front Nine,* off the nightstand and begins reading. She reads for about ten minutes when she begins laughing and says, "My God, a character in this book reminds me of that guy Mickke D I met tonight at Filet's. How funny is that?"

She reaches over on the nightstand, grabs her phone, and calls Page. Page doesn't answer and it goes to voicemail. Connie leaves a message about the character in her book.

తావా

It's almost 12:30 in the morning when Page Rivers arrives at her condo in Little River. She has no attached garage like Connie, so she parks out in the parking lot as close to her building as she can get. She has an assigned parking space but of course, there is a pickup truck parked in her space. The lot is usually fairly well lit, but tonight one of the large parking lot security lights is out. She makes a mental note to call the POA tomorrow to let them know about the light and that someone parked in her spot again. She pulls out Mickke D's business card from her purse and considers writing down the license plate number but it is late and she is tired. She no more than exits her car and takes a few steps toward her building when a voice comes from the direction of the pickup truck. "Hey there, pretty late to be getting in, isn't it?"

The man's voice is garbled and hard to understand. She can hardly make out his figure. She stops and says, "Who are you and what do you want?"

"It's me from earlier this evening, remember?"

As he walks toward her, she sees a man with what looks like sunglasses on, a shaved head and wearing a hip-length leather jacket. He has both hands in his pockets and a big smile on his face. She raises her voice and calls out, "I don't know you and if you don't leave I will scream and call the police."

She reaches in her purse for her whistle but before she can put it to her lips, he has closed the gap between them. He grabs the whistle from her hand and puts his left hand over her mouth. He takes his right hand out of his coat and produces a medium-sized hunting knife which he plunges deep into her mid-section. She feels him turn the blade several times before she blacks out from shock. He catches her as she falls and stabs her several more times.

Within seconds, the attack is over. He lays her body in the back of his truck and covers her with a tarp. He places cinder blocks around the tarp to keep it from blowing around. His next stop is Billybob Swamp. Just as he is leaving the condo complex, a police cruiser pulls into the development. He wonders if someone saw him or if the cruiser is just on a nightly patrol. He drives the speed limit and does not see the cruiser in his rear-view mirror.

On his drive back from the swamp, the hunter keeps muttering to himself, *she should have known better than to treat me that way.*

Chapter 25: Sam and Mickke D

The following Tuesday morning I arrive at my office about 9:45. As I get out of my vehicle and gaze toward the ocean, I see puffy clouds slowly changing shapes as they drift across a vivid blue sky. It's just another beautiful day in paradise. I notice two four-door sedans parked over to one side of my parking lot. One is empty and the other one has two occupants inside. Looks like Detective Concile's cohorts Woolever and Stratten to me. Now what did I do? I wave and go inside. The occupants of the vehicle ignore my wave.

Upon entering the building, Beverly, who looks very sexy today, says to me, "There's a Detective Concile in your office. She said she wants to speak with you. Are you in trouble?"

I get a confused look on my face. "Well, I don't think so but you just never know."

Beverly stands up. "I fixed her a cup of coffee. Would you like me to fix you a cup of tea?"

As I am walking toward my office I say, "That would be great. Bring it down when it's ready."

When you enter my office, my desk is on the left facing the door with two large chairs facing the desk. There is a large window behind my desk and two more large windows, which face the parking area, on the opposite wall facing the door. I can't stand being in a dark office. In an area in front of the door is a medium-sized conference table with four chairs. Detective Concile is staring out into the parking lot with a cup of coffee in her hand. She turns and says to me as I enter, "Must be nice to start your work day at 10. Mine started at 7:30 this morning."

She starts our conversation with a left jab. I counter with a jab of my own. "We have flex hours here, detective. We work as long as it takes to finish the job. What can I help you with today?"

I take a seat at my desk and motion for her to sit. She comes over and sits in one of the oversized stuffed chairs across from me, places her coffee on a coaster on the desk, and crosses her legs. "I think we may have another missing person. Do you know a woman named Page Rivers?"

Before I have a chance to answer, Beverly opens the door and enters with my cup of tea. I thank her and she leaves the office, closing the door on her way out.

"Does she always barge in without knocking?"

My turn to jab. "Only when I ask her to bring my tea when it's ready."

She takes a sip of her coffee and says, "Back to Page Rivers. Do you know her?"

I take a sip of my green tea spiked with a touch of honey. "Not before Saturday night. I met her at Filet's. Why do you think she's missing?"

"We got a call from her employer. When she didn't show up for work on Monday, he sent someone over to check on her. Her car was in the parking lot but she did not answer her door or answer her phone. They talked to her neighbor who just happened to have a key. They went inside but no one was there. The next call was to us."

I butt in. "I thought you did not get involved without a body. Why are you telling me this?"

Her tone of voice never changes. "Let me finish. When the employer was looking around her car, he thought he saw blood on the sidewalk. That's enough to get us involved. Where were you last night between midnight and 1?"

Her question catches me off-guard. "And why in the world would you ask me that question, detective?"

"Mainly because we found your business card lying in the grass next to her car, as well as several drops of blood. We also played her answering machine in her condo and there was a call from a woman named Connie, who mentioned your name along with Filet's. Any wounds on your body, Mickke D?"

I quickly respond. "No detective, but you're more than welcome to look it over if you wish."

She frowns. "That won't be necessary. Tell me about Filet's."

I go into detail about my visit to Filet's and how Page ended up with my business card. I tell her about my four prime suspects and write their names down for her. I also let her know Larry Meggart is number one on my list. I then add that I spent the night with my dog Blue so I have no alibi. I ask her, "So where do we go from here?"

She stands up and replies, "We don't go anywhere. I will look into the matter further and maybe let you know what I find out. Thanks for the coffee. Nice office."

I peer out the window as she says something to Woolever and Stratten and then both cars drive away. I can't, for the life of me, figure out why someone would abduct and maybe kill Page. I need to catch up with the last of my suspects, Terry Graff, and see what his story is.

Chapter 26: Sam and the Suspects

Detective Concile arranges to have all four of the suspects on Mickke D's list come into the station to see if they may have any information on a possible missing persons case. She interviews each one and discovers that none of them could come up with an alibi for Saturday night. They are all divorced, single, and they stated that they went home alone. None of them even has a dog. So far, Mickke D has the best non-alibi, at least his dog can vouch for him.

She has Woolever and Stratten do background checks on the suspects. All four of them moved to the Myrtle Beach area from out west. Larry Meggart is a retired Secret Service agent with a couple of reprimands in his file, nothing serious. Norman Burmiester is a retired Air Force dentist who at one time had a drinking problem. He had several DUIs on his record but again, nothing serious. Seymour Groves is a retired U.S. Postal Service supervisor who was written up for some anger management problems. He attended some classes and had no problems after that. Terry Graff is a retired IRS regional supervisor who was reprimanded for getting into a shouting match with several of his subordinates but he was never written up after that. They have all been divorced at least once, Norman twice. Personally, she doesn't believe any of them is the killer. They just don't seem to fit the profile of a serial killer.

The day after her interviews, she calls Mickke D and updates him on her conclusions. "I don't see any of them as the killer. I think we need to keep looking."

I can't believe my ears. First of all, she actually called me with an update and secondly she used the word, "we" need to keep looking.

I get inquisitive. "So what was your take on Larry Meggart?"

"Just a single, retired Secret Service agent living at the beach. No arrests or domestic violence calls on him since he's been in town. As a matter of fact, he suggested I look at you as a suspect."

"I'll just bet he did." I tell her about my encounter with Mr. Meggart at Night Fever. "I'm still going to keep him at the top of my list."

She replies, "Whatever, just keep me advised if you find something new."

Abruptly and before I can thank her for calling, she hangs up.

Chapter 27: A New Plan

The hunter is on the prowl. It's been almost two weeks since his last venture into Billybob Swamp. He is becoming bored with the restaurant/bar scene and working at his part-time golf course job. It seems as if there are two of him. One who enjoys the chase, the capture, and ending up in bed, and the other one who just enjoys the kill. His latest conquests have not rejected his rather rough pursuit of sex, so he has had no reason to eliminate them, although one of him definitely thought about it.

He is thinking maybe he should start looking for younger prey to pursue. Also, he decides he should move his hunting area farther south, maybe get out of the Little River, Cherry Grove area. He doesn't want to push his luck since he knows that not only the police, but a private investigator, are looking into several missing persons. He can't believe it has taken them this long to start looking for his victims. The papers and news stations have not mentioned anything. It's as if part of him wants to be pursued. He wants an adversary. He decides to find out more about this PI who is asking questions. Maybe the next time he will not discard the body in the swamp.

๛๏๛

Four days later, around 6 a.m., Detective Concile receives a call from her office just as her morning alarm goes off. One of the owners of the Tricia Lynn Motel in Windy Hill found a bloody knife lying in the sand dunes behind the motel and called the police. Sam tells the dispatcher she will skip the office and go directly to the motel.

Sam gets another call just as she is leaving her home. Some early morning walkers on the beach discovered a body in the surf near White Point Swash, which is just south of the Tricia Lynn. The dispatcher tells her they called the coroner along with Woolever and Stratten.

Sam arrives at the Tricia Lynn, takes off her shoes, and walks out to the beach. The sand feels good between her toes. Even though she has lived in the area all of her life, she doesn't get to spend much time at the beach so this is a nice change of pace. It takes her about 10 minutes to get to the swash, during which time she thinks back to a story her mother told her many years ago about how Windy Hill got its name.

It is believed that George Washington scouted out the Southern states during his term, traveling down the King's Highway and he supposedly stayed the night in the vicinity referred to today as Windy Hill. He was walking around the area and his hat blew off. He commented that you should call this place Windy Hill. Her mom said the name stuck and the area is still called Windy Hill today.

When she arrives at the crime scene, the coroner is already there along with Woolever and Stratten. The woman looks as if she is in her mid-thirties, auburn hair, attractive and very dead. She has been stabbed several times in the chest and abdomen. She is fully clothed and the coroner does not think she had been raped or sexually assaulted. He will know more once he gets her back to his office.

Woolever hands Sam the purse he found next to the body and the knife, in a plastic bag, they found behind the motel. He tells Sam they took photos and then wrapped the area with yellow tape. She tells him she saw the tape on her way to the crime scene.

She makes the barefoot, sandy walk back to the motel office, stops by the area where the knife was found, and then meets with the owners of the Tricia Lynn, Don and Margie. Margie is definitely shook up. She spotted the knife when she went to take her early morning walk on the beach and then someone told her about the body being discovered at White Point Swash in the surf. Don tells Sam he may have video of the suspect. He says they have cameras but it was dark when the suspicious activity took place. He shows her the video.

It shows two people walking toward the beach arm in arm, in the beach access area next to the motel. The clock on the video shows 1:38 a.m. The area has lights, but the man's face is hidden by a hat. She does notice he is wearing what looks like a leather, hip-length jacket. The woman does not seem to be resisting and she looks like the dead woman on the beach.

Don makes a copy of the video for her and she heads to her office. On the way, she wonders if this woman could be her fourth missing person, along with Ellen, Jack, and Page, although she really doesn't fit the description. She also wonders if she should call Mickke D. She decides to wait for a while before making that call.

Once at the office, she opens the purse and gets out the victim's wallet. Her name is Jennifer Holmes and she is a local real estate agent. Sam decides to go to the real estate office instead of calling. She takes Woolever and Stratten with her.

They arrive at Sellsmore Realty, introduce themselves to Jan, the receptionist, and ask for the person in charge. They are ushered into Mr. Zink's office, the broker-in-charge, and Sam asks, "Do you have an agent named Jennifer Holmes?"

"Why, yes we do, but she has not shown up today. Is there a problem?"

Sam shows him a photo taken by the coroner. "Oh, my God, yes that's her. What happened, was she in a car accident? Is she all right?"

"Mr. Zink, did she have family here in town?"

"No, she was single and her family lives back in Iowa."

"Mr. Zink, I hate to tell you this but Jennifer was found dead on the beach early this morning."

Chapter 28: Jennifer

Jennifer, along with the other female agents in the office, had been told several times during their weekly meetings to never, ever go on a showing appointment with strangers, and to never go with anyone without first letting someone in the office know where you are going, who you are with, and to always check in with the office to let them know you are okay. They are directed to meet the client at the office, make copies of their driver's license, and to make sure someone else in the office sees them. They should even take another agent along if they are not comfortable with the situation. The office even has code words for the agent to use once they get to the showing to let the office know they are either okay or concerned about who they are with. However, Jennifer was a caring person who always seemed to see the good in people, not the bad. Occasionally, she did not adhere to the rules.

Jennifer was on duty the afternoon the fatal call came in. He sounded innocent enough, although she did have a hard time understanding him. He apologized and stated he had some cough drops in his mouth. He was fighting allergies and a cold. He wanted to see some properties in the Windy Hill area of North Myrtle Beach, particularly one of Jennifer's listings. She thought about it for a minute but since it was getting late, she decided to meet him at her listing, look at some other listings in the area, and then go directly home. She told the caller she would meet him at her listing at 4:30 and then show him a couple other homes in the area.

She had asked the voice on the phone what type of a home he was looking for, style, location, and what price range. She found two other homes in Windy Hill, made copies of the listings and then made calls to the listing agents for showing instructions. She left the office at 4:15, telling Jan she was going to show her listing in Windy Hill, and then go home. She waved, said she would see her tomorrow, and left the office.

She arrived at her listing almost precisely at 4:30. There was a pick-up truck parked in the driveway to the house. A man dressed in blue jeans and a hip-length leather jacket emerged from the pick-up. The man was wearing an Indiana Jones type hat and he had on sunglasses. He took off his hat, revealing a bald, shaved head and introduced himself to her. "Jennifer, I'm Leroy Jefferson, I appreciate you meeting me here on such short notice. You'll have to excuse my voice, the allergies are winning the war."

For just a second, a slight twinge of fear pricks her spine, but the twinge quickly disappears. He doesn't look familiar to her but his voice has somewhat of a recognizable tone to it. She opens the front door of the house and walks in. Leroy follows at a distance, which she feels may be invading her private space. It is a little bit exciting in a weird sort of way. To eliminate her private space phobia, she begins making small talk to try to figure out what this man is looking for or if he is he just a tire kicker.

Moving away from him, she asks, "Are you from this area, Mr. Jefferson?"

Leroy stayed his distance from her and answered, "Oh please call me Leroy and no I'm not. I moved here from out west. How about you, a local?"

Jennifer is very open. "No, I moved here from Iowa. I got tired of the cold weather, snow, and ice up there."

Leroy keeps the conversation going. "How long have you been here, if you don't mind me asking?"

"Oh, about ten years now, I think."

Still holding his hat, he smiles. "You must have been a teenager ten years ago."

Jennifer blushes. She quickly steals a look at his left hand and she notices he is not wearing a wedding ring. Of course, that doesn't mean anything except maybe there's a chance he is not married. She wants to get the conversation back to real estate but so far, that is not working.

Now she asks the magic question. "What about you, Leroy? How long have you been in town? Do you have family here?"

"I've been here about a year now and no family. I'm a widower. My wife died in a car accident."

Jennifer just found out the answer to her question. Now any form of fear is replaced by flowing hormones. She feels an attraction mixed with caution. She tells Leroy she is so sorry to hear about his wife, and then she makes her first mistake. She lets her guard down. After showing him the other homes in the area, Jennifer makes her second mistake; she agrees to have dinner with Leroy to discuss the three homes she had shown him.

శ్రానాం

Leroy makes having dinner such an innocent thing. He only wants to pick her brain for ideas about what type of a house he should buy or maybe should he consider a condo. Jennifer knows better but he seems so honest that she agrees. They go to Rockafellers in Windy Hill for dinner and then on to Dirty Don's at the Marina Inn in Barefoot Resort for drinks. Leroy keeps popping mints; he refers to them as allergy pills. He keeps hinting about going to her place for coffee but Jennifer draws the line in the sand. "Not on the first date," she says.

He controls his anger and around 1:00 in the morning, he asks her if she would like to go for a walk on the beach. She then makes her third and final mistake. She agrees.

With his knife at her throat, and before he kills her, he reminds her that this is the second time she had turned him down. She had told him no at their first meeting. She used the same phrase; "not on the first date." The hunter had met Jennifer at a bar and grille the first month after he had moved here. She was one of the first women to rebuff his advances. Jennifer was on the hunter's list of women who rejected him. He puts a line through her name.

Chapter 29: Sam and Mickke D

After leaving the real estate office, Sam finally gives in and makes the call to Mickke D. "Hey, it's Sam. We found a body on the beach this morning in Windy Hill, but she doesn't fit the description of your missing person."

I am speechless for a second or two. I can't believe she said it was Sam and not Detective Concile and that she is actually calling and offering me information. "Thanks for the update......detective. Do you think they are linked in any way?"

"We don't know much so far, but she was stabbed, not raped or molested, and she was a local real estate agent by the name of Jennifer Holmes."

I am silent for a moment. "I know Jennifer. I did a deal with her a few years back. Seemed like a very nice woman. Any leads?"

"We have the knife and a not-so-good video of the suspect."

She seems more than willing to share information so I ask, "Well, do you mind if I stop by and take a look at the knife and video?"

She hesitates. "No problem, just call me ahead of time."

Many thoughts are now criss-crossing my mind. Is this the same guy who may have killed Ellen, Jack, Connie Smith, and maybe Page? If so, why would he leave the knife? Did he know the camera was there? This is not the work of a very smart and practiced killer who'd left no clues behind before. What is this guy up to? One important lesson I learned as an investigative officer with Army JAG was that most law enforcement officials agree that serial killers usually learn from their mistakes. They evolve. They keep upping the danger and increasing the thrill. This guy is doing just that except it's as if he wants a confrontation. He wants to be pursued.

My investigative juices are flowing. My curiosity is a mix of intrigue and apprehension, my imagination is in overdrive as it desperately tries to put the puzzle together. I can't wait to get to the police station and see the evidence.

☙❧

I call the next morning and meet Sam at the police station an hour later. I say hello to Woolever and Stratten but they are not very receptive to my gesture. I think they are still pissed that I lost them fairly easy when they were tailing me not too long ago. I understand they received a pretty good ribbing from several officers at the station. Oh well, they'll get over it.

Sam takes me into her office and puts the tape in from the Tricia Lynn. She was right; the quality of the video is not that good. No chance of seeing the suspect's face. He seems to be facing away from the camera and talking to his victim. The woman's face is turned toward the camera and is easy to see. I think he knew the camera was there. Sam then shows me the knife. It is just a normal hunting knife probably used to skin an animal. He could have purchased it from any hunting store. My anticipation of the evidence leaves a lot to be desired. There's not much here.

I ask Sam, "So why would he leave the knife? Why not throw it into the ocean or just take it with him? Were there any prints on it?"

"No prints. It was as if he wiped it clean and then dropped it there."

Since she continues to answer, I continue to ask. "Did you find any blood where the knife was found?"

"No, none whatsoever, and the knife was stuck in the sand as if the killer just placed the blade in the sand so that it would be easily found."

"So you think she was killed at the swash and then he brought the knife back to the area behind the public access to the beach?"

"Could be, I really have no clues right now. I am going to send Woolever and Stratten to canvass the area around the house that Jennifer had listed to see if anyone saw the possible suspect with the victim."

"Thanks detective, I'll do some more looking around on my end and if I find out anything I will let you know."

Sam says sarcastically, "Of course you will Mickke D, of course you will."

᭜᭜

Woolever and Stratten talk to everyone who lives within sight of Jennifer's listing. Some people said they remembered seeing some vehicles parked there that day but no one can remember seeing anyone, or exactly what color, or make and model the vehicles were.

Chapter 30: Thomas Alan Cadium

Tuesday morning I'm contemplating my next move with my missing persons case. It seems as if I just can't get motivated to jump into the case with both feet. For some reason I continue to think about Beverly and who she really could be, if not who I think she is. I am also thinking about how nonchalant my life used to be and how I had wished for a more exciting way of life. Well, I got what I wished for but I'm not sure all of this work and possible danger associated with the job is all I expected it to be. Besides that, I'm independently wealthy. On the other hand, maybe I'm just getting old, as one of my old girlfriends Paula Ann said, a "pops."

My phone rings, bringing me back to reality. TC is on the other end and he sounds excited about something. TC, Thomas Alan Cadium, is a retired federal judge and my partner in a treasure salvage venture off the coast of Pawleys Island, along with the state of South Carolina.

I try to sound upbeat. "Hey TC, what's going on at the salvage site?"

"Hey yourself. There's a lot going on down here but I haven't seen you around in a couple of weeks. What's going on your way?"

He's right; I have been shirking my salvage responsibilities. "I've been working on a missing persons case and I just haven't taken the time to come down. Any new discoveries?"

"It seems we find something new every time we go down. I have four assistants assigned to me by Columbia now, all women. They're from England and I think you would them. They're all single and one of them, Stephanie is a tall, well-proportioned woman who fills out a bikini in all the right places. She's about your age and a real knock-out."

Just what I need, another woman in my life. "TC, I have all the problems I need right now with the one I have. Jim thinks

Beverly is either in the Witness Protection Program or in the CIA. My plate is full, but thanks for thinking about my love life. You sound excited, why did you really call?"

He whispers, "Mickke D, I found a treasure map at the wreck site along with the ship's logbook."

"Now wait a minute TC, the last map I got involved in with you got several people killed and almost you and me."

"Well if you're not interested, I can probably find someone else who enjoys looking for buried treasure."

I hesitate for a few seconds and I just know TC is laughing on the other end of the phone. I finally say, "Let me ask you this. I thought everything we found at the site was the property of the State of South Carolina?"

"Well, I guess that depends on how you interpret the agreement. I think that only means treasure found in the ocean, at the wreck site."

"Didn't you just tell me you found the map in the ocean at the wreck site?"

"Yes, I did, but a map is not considered treasure. A map may or may not be worth anything. And if the map is right, the treasure is buried on land, not in the ocean at the wreck site."

"Okay, you're the lawyer; you guys are good at spinning things to benefit yourselves. Tell me what you discovered."

He continues, "I was on the outside of the ship and my four assistants were working inside when I brushed up against what I thought was just a branch sticking out of the sand. I went to break it off so no one else would run into it and as I was moving the sand, I noticed it was a container of some sort, about eighteen inches long with wooden stoppers in both ends. I'm going to guess the water swelled the wood and sealed the container. When I got home I dug out the wooden stoppers and low and behold, there was a ships logbook wedged inside and when I opened the logbook, I found the map."

"So where is the treasure buried?" I sarcastically ask.

"Well, therein lies the problem. It could be anywhere along the coast. Somehow we need to find out what the coastline along the Grand Strand, looked like in the late 1600s and early 1700s. I've looked at current coastline maps and don't see anything that resembles anything on my map. Got any ideas?"

I think about that for a few seconds and I do come up with an idea but I want TC to stew for a while. "Not right now. What's our timetable on this?"

"Well, if it's been buried since the late 1600s or early 1700s, I guess it's not going anywhere real soon. Call me back when you want to see the map and let me know when you're coming down to meet my new helpers. I told them about you and they said they can't wait to meet you."

"Okay TC. I'll meet the girls later. Why don't you come up here for lunch and bring your map with you. However, whatever you do, don't mail it to me. I remember what happened to the last guy you mailed a map."

"No problem, Mickke D. No more mailing maps for me."

Chapter 31: Stephanie

The only reason Stephanie and her team want to meet Mickke D is to size up the enemy. Stephanie Langchester is a British subject as are the other three members of her handpicked team. She has a degree in marine biology and she worked for British Intelligence for six years. She is forty-eight years old and decided she was never going to get the things in life she wanted by being honest. She read in the British tabloids about a discovery off the coast of South Carolina and figured this may be her chance to begin her drive toward illegal wealth. She put together her team and offered her services to the State of South Carolina at no charge. She only asked for room and board plus expenses for her and her team. What a deal. The state took her up on her offer and assigned her and her team to TC. Right away, she knew TC was not going to be a problem but she isn't sure about Mickke D. From the way TC described him, he could be trouble.

Stephanie does not consider herself a bad person. Actually, she was at the top of her class her entire life. She loved being a marine biologist and her stint with British Intelligence taught her how to spot the good guys from the bad guys. It also provided a look inside the criminal mind and a clear picture of what made those people tick. She also discovered where they went wrong and why they were caught. She started to realize that she could probably pull off a heist and not be arrested. Her plan was to steal something that really didn't belong to anyone and hurt no one along the way. However, if push comes to shove, she will be ready to do whatever it takes to complete the job because this caper is going to be the beginning of her retirement plan, which means she will never have to work again at a real job.

The only problem with her plan was that she needed help to pull off the caper. She knows that anytime you involve other people, there is a chance of failure, it only takes one weak link, but her plan was too big to pull off by herself. She was going to need help.

Her handpicked team consists of Pat Livingrock, a fellow marine biologist; Jenny Blare, a former British Intelligence agent who left the service under questionable circumstances; and Karen Bruogg, a former professional golfer on the Women's European Golf Tour. They all, just like Stephanie, enjoy the better things in life. They all like fine wine, and they love to party on the French and Italian rivieras. They all like fast cars and dangerous men. They love adventure and pushing the envelope. It is Stephanie's job to meld this group into a lean, mean, stealing machine and to make sure all of the links are strong.

രംഷ

Stephanie was just coming out of the buried ship as TC was making his discovery of the container holding the logbook. From behind the ship, she saw TC gather up the container and carry it to the surface.

Now, I wonder what that could be, she thinks to herself.

When they get back to the surface and on the salvage boat, TC asks Stephanie, "So, did you find anything different and exciting this time?"

She answers with a question of her own. "No, mainly the same kind of stuff. What about you, anything new on your end?"

He hesitates and then answers her. "No, not really."

Stephanie smiles and thinks to herself, *Yeah right, we'll see about that.*

Chapter 32: Mickke D & Bess

TC calls me the next day and says he'll come up tomorrow with the map and the logbook. I tell him to come to my office, then we'll have lunch and we'll decide what we're going to do about his new acquisition. I tell him not to say a word about my thoughts on Beverly. He has met her several times so she is not a stranger. In fact, now that I think about it, she was very inquisitive about my relationship with TC. Maybe she's with the IRS and not the CIA.

I get on the phone and call an acquaintance, Bess Long, who owns My Sister's Bookstore in Pawleys Island. A friend of mine, D.G. Snipes, wrote a book *The Raider Christian Jack*, and I went with him to a book signing at her bookstore. That was where I first met Bess. She confided in me that she had a large cache of old maritime maps that one of her girlfriends' great-grandfather had acquired years and years ago. At the time, I didn't think much about it but now I am wondering if any of those old maps could possibly help TC locate his buried treasure.

"Hey Bess, its Mickke D, D.G. Snipes' friend from his book signing."

She sounds perky. "Oh sure Mickke D, I remember you, tall, hunkish, and single. Didn't I introduce you to several of my single girlfriends that day?"

"Well, I don't know about the hunkish part, is that even a word? But the tall and single part is correct. And yes you introduced me to some of your friends, but that's not why I'm calling."

Her voice changes from perky to serious. "Sorry, what can I help you with?" She sounds as if all the air was just let out of her balloon. Maybe she enjoys playing matchmaker.

"Actually I'm calling about those old maritime maps you said you had in your storage room. Would there be any chance of looking at them someday when I'm in your part of the world?"

Her voice becomes perky again. "Sure, anytime. Just call me so I can dig them out. They're back in a corner somewhere. As a matter of fact, I can have my girlfriend Susan here, the one who gave me the maps."

I pause and then say, "Don't tell me, she's single and available?"

She quickly replies, "Mickke D, it's strictly a coincidence, but maybe we could all have lunch together, your treat."

I figure I have no choice so I answer, "Sounds great Bess, I'll call a day in advance. Nice talking with you again."

Just for giggles and chuckles, I wait maybe 30 seconds and call the bookstore again. The line is busy. I wonder with whom she is talking. All of a sudden, it is as if everyone along the Grand Strand is concerned about my love life. I wonder if there isn't a single women's club out there somewhere and their job is to find out who is available and if they're well off. Oh well, I guess TC and I can force ourselves to take a couple of nice-looking young ladies to lunch. After all, it's for a good cause, the quest for buried treasure.

Chapter 33: The Map

TC pulls into the office around 11 a.m. He says hello to Beverly and she ushers him back to my office. I close the door, put my ear to the door, and listen for Beverly's footsteps to disappear down the hallway. I would have never considered doing that or even closing my door before my conversation with Jim at R.W. Woods.

"So Mickke D, where are we having lunch?"

"I was thinking maybe Boulineau's salad bar. We'll eat upstairs where it's quiet. And by the way, your treat."

"Sounds good to me. Do you want to look at the map before we go or afterward?"

I notice a briefcase in his hand and say, "Let's take it with us. We can look at everything after we have lunch. By the way, I hope that's not the original case or I can tell you right now it's a fake."

He laughs. "Oh, no, the original container is at home. It started to deteriorate as soon as I got it out of the water. Are you sure you want me to take it along? I was just going to leave it here or in my car while we had lunch."

I hesitate. "Just to be safe, let's take it with us."

We say good-bye to Beverly as we exit the office and opt to walk down to Boulineau's, which is only three or four blocks away. As we leave, Beverly has a funny look on her face, as if to say, "why aren't you inviting me to come along?"

I introduced TC to Boulineau's months ago, and now he loves it as much as I do. Frank and Louise Boulineau opened a small mom and pop grocery store in 1948 in Cherry Grove Beach, which would later become a part of North Myrtle Beach. There were less than 100 homes in Cherry Grove at the time. The store has been expanded several times and now contains 80,000 square feet of shopping on two floors with glass elevators and many specialty departments, including a food court and cafeteria. The expanded space has created a truly unique shopping complex as well as one of the area's most recognizable landmarks, the Boulineau's Lighthouse. They have one of the freshest and best salad bars around with great homemade soups. To go along with the IGA grocery complex, there is a gas station, car wash, and a hardware store, which includes a sportsman's center and a post office. The ultimate in one-stop shopping.

We take our lunch upstairs where it is usually a lot less congested than downstairs. TC opts for the vegetable soup and I choose the chicken noodle for starters.

"So TC, what makes you think the map and logbook are authentic?"

"Just wait till you see them, you'll understand, but right now eat your lunch. I can't wait to show it to you."

We take turns going downstairs to fill up our plates with salad and all the fixings. TC does not want to leave his booty alone. Neither one of us go back for seconds. TC knows he has me hooked and he is relishing the moment. A lady comes around and picks up our empty trays and dishes and cleans off our table. TC looks around the room and then opens his briefcase and pulls out what looks like a large sealable plastic bag with a brown book-like object inside. He gently pulls the book from its hiding place.

Chapter 34: The Logbook

The logbook, I'm going to guess, is about six by nine, and is bound in what looks like leather with three rusty metal brads. I can see it is pliable and you can tell it has been rolled up. As soon as it emerges from the bag, I can smell the staleness; that odor which says, *I am old, treat me with respect.*

TC is holding the book as if he is holding a small bird, firm enough to keep it from flying away, but not so hard as to harm it. It's almost as if he is having an intimate relationship with the book.

He looks directly at me and in a very subdued voice, he says, "Do you know that the last person to touch this book before me probably was the man who wrote it, maybe 300 years ago?"

Wow, this is heavy. Actually, I had not thought about that, but now that he mentions it, this is cool. "So what does it say and where is the map?" I ask. I'm starting to get excited and at the same time irritated.

"In time Mickke D, in time. You can't rush history. You need to savor the moment."

I raise my voice and say, "Oh come on TC, tell me what's in the damn book."

He smiles and I can tell he is messing with me. He knows he has me hook, line, and sinker.

He begins speaking slowly, "I have read this through at least a dozen times and it is unbelievable. The ship was the Queen Beth and she was British. Her captain was Captain Kent Swinely and it appears as if he was on a mission that today we would consider as being covert.

"The Queen Beth was not flying a British flag but an independent flag from an unknown nation. Captain Swinely's job was to intercept pirate ships and take whatever booty she may have in her belly, kill all hands on board, and sink the ship. The world would think another pirate ship had done the deed and not the British.

"As The Queen Beth began filling her belly with gold, silver, and treasure, the men on board, who were not British sailors, became more and more difficult to control and prone toward mutiny. Captain Swinely heard them talking several times about taking over the ship, killing him and splitting up the treasure on board.

"One evening while the ship was anchored offshore, he gives all hands the night off and tells them not to return until the next day. He figures they will all get stinking drunk and end up in the nearest brothel.

"Captain Swinely finds and hires three men to help him remove the treasure, except for one chest full of coins. He offers them a fair wage and he gives each of them a bottle of rum. They make several trips with the accumulated treasure aboard a long boat, and bury it on shore. From the way he describes the episode, it was an all night-affair and his helpers ended up very drunk. Once they had accomplished their goal and placed the last of the treasure in the open tomb, he kills all of his help and throws their bodies into the same burial place as the treasure. Now only he knows where the treasure resides. He covers the treasure and the bodies, and returns to the ship.

"He then draws a crude map to the buried booty and places it in his logbook. When his men return to the ship late the next day, they never realize the treasure is gone. Captain Swinely had transferred the treasure into canvas bags before it left the ship and the men filled more canvas bags with rocks to bring back to the ship. He filled the empty chests with rocks to weigh about what they weighed before he emptied them. He placed the locked chests filled with rocks along with the one chest filled with coins, in the ships galley and covered them with canvas. He had to keep the coins because he paid the men out of the chest of coins. Everything looked the same as when the men left. Two days later, April 4, 1705, Captain Swinely makes his last entry. The Queen Beth is under attack from two different pirate ships and she is going down. The captain's last sentence in the book is that he will try to keep his logbook safe."

I am speechless. I open my mouth to speak but nothing comes out. This is totally cool. I finally ask a question, "Where were they when they buried the treasure?"

TC shakes his head and answers, "I don't know, the captain never mentions a specific location, but it has to be near some port on the coast and within two days sailing from where we found the ship. But it would depend on the winds, the ocean currents, and which direction he was going when the ship was attacked."

TC turns to a page in the logbook and pulls out a folded piece of parchment. He opens it and hands it to me. I am half-afraid to touch it but it seems to be in good shape. It is a very simple drawing. I can make out the coastline, a ship, and a river, a creek, or an inlet. On one side of the river or creek, it shows what looks to be buildings, which may be a town or port, and on the other side of the creek, river, or inlet some wavy lines, which could be a hill, a pond, or a lake. There is an X above the wavy lines. I'm going to guess that is the point where the captain buried the treasure.

I carefully hand the map back to TC and he places it back in the logbook and then without uttering a word, he places the book back into the plastic bag and then into his briefcase.

Finally, he turns to me and says, "So Mickke D, where do we go from here?"

"Well, TC let me ask you this. Does he mention any locations at all in the logbook?"

"The writing is very difficult to read but the only location he mentions in the logbook is Charles Towne, which later became Charleston. He mentions other places but I think they are either swashes or creeks. I couldn't find any matching names on any maps from Little River, all the way down to Charleston."

"Okay TC, here's the down and dirty. I know a woman at a bookstore in Pawleys Island who has some very old maps and she said we could take a look at them. She just wants me to call her ahead of time and let her know we are coming. Oh, and by the way, we have to buy her and her girlfriend lunch."

"Sounds like a fair exchange to me, when do you want to go?"

"Well, since you have to go back that way today, maybe we can look at them this afternoon and we'll buy the girls dinner instead of lunch."

Without hesitation he replies, "Let's do it. You can call her when we get back to your office."

I pause. My mind switches to Beverly. "No, I think I'll call her right now, from here."

I make the call. Bess agrees and we set a time to meet. Maybe I'll get lucky and her girlfriend won't be able to make it on such short notice. I tell TC how to get to the bookstore and tell him I'll meet him there at 3 p.m. If he gets there first, I instruct him to ask for Bess. We both arrive at about the same time.

Chapter 35: Bess and Susan

Bess is her usual jovial self and all smiles. She introduces us to her sister Fran, who reads all of the books in the store so that they can be classified as used. And of course, I was wrong about the girlfriend not being able to make it on short notice. Bess introduces us to her girlfriend, Susan Heinz Belmont, whose great-grandfather acquired the maps. Susan looks to be about Bess's age, mid to late-thirties. She is a very attractive woman with short blond hair and glasses. She has that sexy school teacher look to her, almost looks like the English teacher I had a crush on in high school who I wished would make me stay after class and write on the board 1,000 times, *sorry I kept staring at my teacher when I should have been reading*. She even has the same first name, Susan. I think I even named a cat after her several years later, Susie Q.

I snap out of my daze and ask Bess if we can see the maps. She takes us back to a rather small storeroom in the rear of the building. My daze returns. In these close quarters, Susan's perfume even smells like that high school English teacher I had a crush on.

I opt to start a conversation and acquire more information about the maps from her. "Susan, how did your great-grandfather end up with the maps?"

She answers but I only hear the sounds and not the words. Her voice has a melodic, medium throaty sound to it, and I can feel perspiration beads pop up on my forehead. It is getting very warm in this small room. I don't understand how I am able to break someone's arm, leg, or neck and maybe even kill them without a second thought, but when it comes to women, I just give in. I seem to have no self-control. No wonder I've been married, divorced, and broke three times.

Before she has a chance to complete her answer, Bess says, "Here they are, back here behind this cabinet."

Bess places the roll of maps on a small table covered with paperbacks. She looks at Susan and says, "Let's go back up front and let these guys look at these old smelly maps on their own. Besides, we need to figure out where they are taking us for dinner."

I sigh as I watch Susan and Bess leave. TC carefully unrolls the maps and we begin to try to find something, anything that looks remotely like the location on the logbook map.

We spend almost an hour going over the maps and we come up with several possibilities. The best possibility looks like a part of Hobcaw Barony, next to Winyah Bay, but we both realize we are looking for a needle in a haystack. TC goes up front and asks if he can make drawings of the maps and Susan tells him to go ahead and take the maps, as long as he promises to return them to the bookstore. Of course, TC agrees.

We take the girls over to The Hammock Shops and walk around the complex before stopping at Nosh for dinner. During our walk, I get that feeling again that someone is watching us, and yet I spot no one who looks suspicious. After a great dinner, we stop in The Original Hammock Shop so Bess can say hello to Denny and check out the competition in the bookshop arena. She seems impressed with their selection. Before Bess can suggest anything else to do for the evening, I thank them for their help and state that I enjoyed dinner and their company but I need to get back to Little River. Bess nudges Susan and she pulls a business card from her purse and hands it to me. Of course, I give her one of mine. I leave TC with the girls and venture back north to my office. TC promises to call me if he finds anything interesting in the maps.

Chapter 36: Jimmy Bruce

Wednesday morning. I no sooner get into the office and my phone rings.

I don't recognize the number and almost let it go to voicemail but since this is a real estate office and it could be a perspective client, I finally pick up. "Mickke D Real Estate, this is Mickke D. How can I help you?"

"Yes, my name is Jimmy Bruce. I wonder if someone in your office might show me a condo at The Village at the Glens. I'm looking for a nice condo and I'm willing to pay cash. I have the address if that helps."

I have a very hard time understanding him. It is as if he has a mouth full of pebbles. "I'll be happy to show you the listing, Mr. Bruce. What is the address and when would you like to see it?"

He gives me the address. "How about one o'clock this afternoon? I'm leaving town on Friday and I would like to have some ideas before I leave town."

"Sure, let me find the listing and call the agent to see if I can set something up for you. Should I call you back at this number?"

The caller hesitates and then answers. "No, I'm at a convenience store pay phone. I'll just be at the condo at one and if you don't show up, I'll just figure you could not make arrangements."

It sounds strange to me that he would not have a cell phone but I have met some strange people looking for homes and condos who are very well off.

I confirm the address with him and hang up. I find the condo and call the listing agent. She tells me the unit is unoccupied, and there is no problem with showing it at 1 p.m. I make copies of the listing to give to Mr. Bruce.

I arrive at The Village at the Glens about 12:45 to open up the unit, turn the lights on, and preview the condo before Mr. Bruce arrives. The building looks familiar to me. It's just like the one that Jack Miller was staying in and it is only one building away. I am about to use my real estate key to open the lock box when I am startled by a loud voice directly behind me. "Hey, Mr. PI. Are you looking for another missing person?"

It's Ray, the condo manager. I uncoil and relax. "No, just showing this unit to a client at 1. Say, did you ever hear from your friend Jack?"

"No, not a peep. What about you? Did you ever find him?"

Ray had no more than finished his question when a shot rings out and Ray falls to the ground. I can tell by the blank look on his face he is dead. I duck behind a car. Terror grips my heart. Every one of my senses is telling me that danger is nearby. I reach for my .45 in the small of my back, but I never have my weapon on me at a real estate showing or listing. The .45 is in the car and it is about thirty feet away from me. I am alone, with no weapon in a large parking lot and I have no idea where the shot came from. This is not good.

I grab my cell phone and dial 911. I tell the operator my name and location and ask her to send the police and the EMTs, although I think the guy is dead. I am still waiting for the shooter to fire again or just walk up and shoot me. I hear nothing but silence.

Several condo doors open and I yell at the people to go back inside. I pop my head up slowly and look around the area. There is another building to my left and what looks like a large wooded area directly behind the building. Looks like a great location for a shooter. I position myself so that the car is between the wooded area and me. Minutes seem like hours, but I still hear nothing but silence.

Finally, I stand up and go to my vehicle. If he were going to attack me, he would have already done so. I grab my .45 from the console and run toward the wooded area. As I reach the edge of the woods, I stop and crouch down. My demons are returning and I know I should pursue the enemy and eliminate him.

My eyes are as alert as a Doberman's, scouring the woods as it encloses me, my gun leading the way. I look for signs that he was here. Before long, I find broken branches, underbrush which has been trampled down, and the smell of gunpowder is still in the air. I turn toward the parking lot and find a clean line of sight to where Ray was standing. This is where he fired the shot. I mark the spot with one of my business cards, which I wedge into a branch. Sirens bring me back to reality. I am not in the jungle; I am in Little River, South Carolina. I walk out of the woods and get almost to my vehicle as the EMTs arrive. Within minutes, the police show up. Woolever and Stratten get out of the first vehicle and of course, Detective Concile arrives seconds later. She gets out and begins shaking her head before a word is ever spoken. "Mickke D, you never fail to amaze me."

I have a blank look on my face. "I know detective, we need to stop meeting this way."

"So who shot this guy and isn't he the same guy that was with you at Mr. Miller's condo?"

"Yeah, same guy, Ray Bonsai." I go over everything that took place and tell her that I marked the place in the woods where I think the ambush took place with my business card.

She turns toward me and says, "And why do you think it was an ambush?"

I tell her about the phone call and the showing appointment with Jimmy Bruce. I can't believe I didn't see this coming. "The whole thing was a set-up but I don't understand why he shot Ray and not me."

"Mickke D, someone out there doesn't like you and they're trying to send you a message."

Sam tells Woolever and Stratten to go into the woods, find where I marked the possible location of the shooter, and see what they can find. She watches as the coroner shows up and takes the body away. She turns to me and says, "Mickke D, you're in danger. If I were you I would be very careful from now on."

Instantaneously I think of a quote I heard on TV the other night. "No detective, I'm not in danger. I *am* the danger. No problem. I'll keep my eyes wide open and my head down. Do you think this has anything to do with the missing persons case?"

"Well, if it was the Colombians, they would have shot you, not Mr. Bonsai. Anyone else have a beef with you besides your ex-wives?"

I give her a wry smile and reply, "No, but I have had the funny feeling that someone has been watching me for the last couple of weeks. Maybe, it was this guy. We need to find him before he kills again."

She points her finger at me. "No Mickke D, *I'll* find him. You go back to selling real estate and planting posies or whatever it is you do, and be sure to come down to the station and give me a written statement. You know the drill."

I give her a cold stare. "Detective, he just made it personal today. He crossed the line. He is now my first priority. I'll let you know if I find out anything."

I guess she knows better than to try to change my mind. She just turns away and goes over to where Woolever and Stratten are combing the area for evidence, but then she stops, turns around and says, "Good luck and please keep me advised."

కొన

The hunter's plans had been changed. He had originally just planned to intimidate Mickke D, maybe shoot out his back window, but when a target arrived on the scene, he decided to give him a real scare. He didn't know the man he shot but he seemed to know Mickke D, so wrong time, wrong place, too bad. He only fired one shot, then folded up his rifle, returned it to its case and casually walked out of the woods on the far side of the building from the attack. He was leaving the development just as the authorities were arriving. He is thinking to himself, *this is almost too easy.*

೭ಿ೭ಿ

Detective Sam Concile is starting to get concerned that she and her team are getting nowhere with the investigation of the missing persons and the murders of Jennifer Holmes and now Ray Bonsai. They have talked to and interviewed hundreds of witnesses and possible suspects. They need someone to come forward and give them even the smallest piece of evidence and a possible description. She is also concerned that Mickke D may be the killer's next victim; however, he just may be lucky enough to get the killer before the killer gets him. She also figures that if that happens, the killer will be dead and there will be no trial and no cost to the taxpayers. That would be fine with her.

She opts to send Woolever and Stratten, undercover, out to several of the bars and restaurants in the Little River, North Myrtle Beach area and see what they can find out. Maybe they'll get lucky and stumble across someone who knows something.

After several weeks and many nights hitting the bars and clubs in the Little River and North Myrtle Beach area, Woolever and Stratton come up empty. Sam has to pull them from the gig because the chief of police won't authorize any more overtime. Sam is right back where she started, nowhere.

Chapter 37: The Boat Ride

Even though I am independently wealthy, I am also aware that play toys sometimes take up a lot of valuable time. Since TC got me back on the water, my temperature for owning a boat began to rise. However, the thought of taking care of it lowered my temperature in a big hurry. I always thought boating should be an escape, not a nuisance, so I figured out a way to have my cake and eat it too. I joined The Freedom Boat Club in North Myrtle Beach. It was sort of like joining a country club. I paid an initiation fee and then a monthly fee. I enjoy the boat and they take care of it, and I have access to boats all over the country.

Beverly calls and suggests we do a waterway cruise on Saturday, which is what we used to do most Saturdays as long as the weather was good. I agree since the weather forecast is for sunny and warm. We normally try to leave the Harborgate Marina by the swing bridge around 10 in the morning. Beverly packs a picnic lunch while I provide sodas, beer, and a chilled bottle of wine. We usually return to the marina by 1 in the afternoon.

This will be my first time out with Beverly since the episode on the boardwalk and my encounter at The Village at the Glens in Heather Glen. We have confined our time together to her place or mine with an occasional dinner before or a pizza after. Things have been rather quiet between us since Jim gave me his assessment of my choice in girlfriends.

Chris, Paul, and Karen are in the office when I go to pick up my boat. I choose a 32-foot Chris Craft with twin 350 motors named U-Betcha. It's a great boat for a waterway cruise.

Karen takes us down to the boat and, as usual, it is spotless and ready to go. She tells us the tide is coming in so we can go just about anywhere we wish. We load up our food and drinks and venture up the waterway toward Little River. I usually don't bring my weapon with me on our boat trips, but today at the last minute, I decide to bring it along. I put it on ice in the cooler in a plastic bag.

What a beautiful day in paradise, warm, sunny, and very little boat traffic. We are in no hurry, just enjoying the boat ride and the great weather. It is nice to be out here on the water and forget about the fact that someone may be trying to kill me. Of course, I am having a hard time not thinking about who Beverly may really be, but when she takes off her shorts and shirt and reveals this really small black bikini, all of a sudden that thought is replaced by other thoughts.

We cruise slowly up the waterway. The Atlantic Intercoastal Waterway is a "toll free canal" which affords continuous protected passage behind the Atlantic coast to the Florida Keys for more than 1,243 statute miles from Norfolk, Virginia, to Key West, Florida. It provides for at least a depth of 12 feet from Norfolk to Fort Pierce, Florida, thence 10 feet to Miami and then 7 feet to Key West. During World War II, the route became important as a means of avoiding German submarines along the Atlantic coast.

Being in real estate, I also realize that the waterway made quite a few landowners very rich. It has provided a location for hotels, resorts, golf courses, marinas, and million-dollar homes. Beverly and I enjoy looking at all the sights along the way.

As we cruise north, we pass Capt. Poo's, Cedar Creek and Lightkeepers Village, Coquina Harbour, Eastport, Tidewater, Rivergate, Snookey's, Mariners Point, Crab Catchers, Glen Dornoch Golf Course, Wind Jammer Village, Big Landing and then out the Little River Inlet to the Atlantic Ocean. We hug the coast of Waites Island south to Hog Inlet. We beach the boat across from Cherry Grove Point, have lunch on the beach, sun ourselves for about an hour, and head back the same way we came.

The cruise back is equally enjoyable until we get to the Coquina Harbour Marina. Just as we pass the opening to the marina, we hear the roar of boat engines and within seconds, a boat speeds out from the marina and almost crashes into our boat. Beverly screams and I turn our Chris Craft abruptly to avoid a collision. The boat that almost hit us is a 30-foot Contender with three 250 Yamaha motors on the rear. The driver of the other boat has a poncho covering his body and head. I cannot make out his face, just that he has on sunglasses. He slows his boat about 50 yards away from us and yells out, "You want some of this? Come on."

I give him the finger, yell some obscenities, and consider reaching for my weapon, but cooler heads prevail for now.

Beverly says, "What is that asshole trying to do, sink us?"

I reply as I point to my beverage cooler. "I'm not sure, but my .45 is in that cooler. Do you know how to use it?"

She nonchalantly replies, "Sure. I've taken some shooting classes."

For some reason, that answer does not surprise me. "Okay, so get the gun out but don't start shooting unless I tell you to or if he starts shooting at us."

I'm starting to wonder if this could be the same guy who killed Ray at Heather Glen, just some weekend boater who has had too much to drink or maybe the person who I think has been watching me for several weeks. I wonder why he is wearing a poncho to cover up his identity. It's much too warm for that attire.

I ease the Chris Craft forward slowly to see what his intentions are and as I do, I hear Beverly pull the slide on my .45. I turn toward her and she says with a smile, "I'm ready. Just point, relax and pull the trigger. Is that right?"

"Yeah, right." I turn back toward our adversary. I give our boat some more throttle and when I get to within maybe 30 yards of him, he yells out, "Maybe next time Mickke D, maybe next time."

He guns his Contender. I know I have no chance of catching him but I slam the Chris Crafts throttle forward and the thrust of the engine knocks Beverly down and the .45 goes off.

I shut the boat down. I don't feel any pain anywhere on my body and I don't see any blood, so I guess she missed me.

"Why didn't you tell me it had a hair trigger on it?" she screams as she gets up from the deck floor and hands the gun to me.

I look around and see a large hole in the side of the Chris Craft just above the water line. I wonder if bullet holes are covered in my insurance coverage at The Freedom Boat Club.

By the time we get going again, the Contender is out of sight. I nurse U-Betcha back to the Harborgate Marina. We are unpacking the boat as Karen walks down to the dock. I tell Beverly that I will do the explaining. Karen climbs onboard and asks us how the trip was.

"Well, I guess you might say it had its moments." I point to the hole in the side of the Chris Craft.

"My God, what did you run into?" she exclaims.

"Well, actually Beverly was holding my gun when I took off too fast. She fell down and the gun went off."

"Are both of you all right?"

"Yes, we're fine. Does my insurance cover this?"

Karen looks perplexed. "Well, I don't know. I'll have to talk to Chris and Paul. I don't think we have ever had a claim for a bullet hole in one of our boats before. I'm just glad the two of you are okay."

Chris and Paul don't seem that concerned and tell me they will e-mail Carl, their insurance agent, and if there's a problem, they'll get back to me.

On the way back to Beverly's condo, she asks, "Who was that guy and what was he trying to do?"

"Oh, I think he was just a novice weekend boater who had too much to drink."

She gives me a strange look. "So then why was he wearing a poncho on such a warm day, and why did he know your name?"

Chapter 38: The Hunter

The hunter has done his homework. Since his shooting encounter with Mickke D at The Village at The Glens, he has been following him whenever he has time. He has always kept a safe distance so as not to be seen. He knows pretty much what he does and when he does it. Now it's time to get his attention again. He plans to play with him just as a cat plays with a mouse before he lunges for the kill. He wants to aggravate him. One thing that has stuck out to him is that he has been taking his lady friend boating on Saturdays. Same time each morning and they usually stay out on the water for about the same time each trip. They have not been out for several weeks, so he thinks they are about due. He is watching.

The hunter has been checking the want ads for boats for sale and he has found one just south of the swing bridge, close to where Mickke D has his boat. It is a 30-foot Contender with three 250 Yamaha motors which has been for sale for quite awhile. He told the owner he would come by and take it out for a ride soon, maybe on very short notice. When the time is right, he will send Mickke D a message on the waterway. Nothing fatal yet, just another warning shot across the bow.

∿●∿

The hunter is sitting in his pick-up truck on the other side of the waterway from The Harborgate Marina with his binoculars, watching for any sign of Mickke D. A little after 10 he sees Mickke D and his girlfriend walk down to the dock toward the boats. He watches as they leave the marina and head north up the waterway toward Little River.

He knows they will not return for at least two hours so he waits for an hour before calling the guy with the boat for sale.

He tells him he is on his way over to take the boat for a spin. The owner of the boat says okay and to come on over. The hunter has a backpack with him, which has a poncho in it. He gives the boat owner a hundred dollar bill as a deposit for gas for the boat. He cruises up the waterway to Coquina Harbour and waits for Mickke D to return. It's time to turn up the heat a little bit. He changes into the lightweight poncho.

After putting a scare into Mickke D and his friend and as he is leaving the area, he hears a shot but he can't believe Mickke D would fire at him in broad daylight from a moving boat. He looks behind him and Mickke D is not following him. He is dead in the water. He changes back into his every day clothes and returns the boat to the dock. He tells the owner he likes the boat and that he will get back to him.

Now it's time to plan his next move.

Chapter 39: Senator Brazile

Senator Brazile puts in a call to an old acquaintance of his on Grand Cayman Island in the Bahamas. Maurice Seaton is the head of the International Banking Cartel, which is headquartered on Grand Cayman. The senator met Maurice in Atlanta at a banking conference several years ago where the senator was the keynote speaker. Maurice lobbied the senator to kill a bill which would limit the privacy of offshore numbered bank accounts. The bill never made it out of committee. Maurice made a substantial donation to the senator's re-election campaign fund and told him if he ever needed anything down his way to be sure and let him know.

The senator makes the call. "Maurice, Senator Brazile here. I'm calling to take you up on your offer."

Maurice sounds surprised. "Of course, senator. How can I help you?"

"I would like to know if a certain person has an account on Grand Cayman and if they do, where is the account located and what is the balance. Do you think you can help me with that?"

Maurice thinks about it for a few seconds. "Give me the name of the person and I'll get back to you." The senator gives him Connie Smith's name and also adds her social security number.

Maurice calls him back forty-five minutes later. "The account in question is at the Cayman National Trust Bank and the balance is $765,422.13 and it was a cash deposit."

Since he knows Connie was an only child with no children, he asks Maurice, "What happens to the money in the account in the event the person is killed or dies and there are no heirs?"

Maurice hesitates for a few seconds. "The money would go into a trust fund and would be controlled by a trustee appointed by the bank."

Senator Brazile thinks for a minute. "And what would be the odds of the bank appointing me as the trustee?"

"I would think the odds would be very good, senator."

Maurice is smiling on the other end of the phone. If this scenario works out the way he thinks it will work out, he will have a United States senator in his back pocket.

But this is not Senator Brazile's first rodeo. He is taping the phone call and since it is a federal offense to give out information about numbered offshore bank accounts, if he goes down, so will Maurice. The senator considers it a draw and just a cost of doing business.

Chapter 40: The Wine Festival

True fear is a gift. It is a survival signal that alerts you only in the presence of danger. Fear can also be an ally. I have learned to always take it with me, no matter what or where the fight. I had it with me in the jungles of Colombia and I still have it even now, on the streets of Myrtle Beach.

I am sitting with Beverly at La Belle Amie Vineyard in Little River, relaxing with a beer and listening to great music being played by an oldies band. Beverly is having a glass of wine and basking in the warm afternoon sun.

All of a sudden, the hair on the back of my neck is doing flip-flops, just like the night when I was leaving Filet's and I felt as if someone was watching or stalking me. It's the same feeling I have had for the last several weeks that someone has been watching me.

I immediately get up from my folding chair and rest my back against a tree, which is next to where we are sitting. I slowly touch my chrome-plated .45, which is holstered in the small of my back, covered by my shirt. This eases a little bit of my anxiety.

We are seated about one-third of the way down a shallow incline in a natural ampitheater, where the band is located. I survey the crowd below me. There are at least 1,000 people here today because it is one of the last concerts of the year. No one seems to be looking my way, let alone caring what I am doing. They have all brought their favorite outdoor lounge chairs with them. The chairs are comfortable and have room to place a beer, bottle of wine, or a glass filled with their favorite beverage. Some of the patrons have ice buckets for their white wine and others just have a bottle of red sitting next to their chair.

My panic mode is rising to the high-water mark and still climbing. It is time to move. My apprehension and imagination is in overdrive as I try to find the source of my unwarranted predicament.

I tell Beverly I am going to the restroom and that I'll be right back. I opt not to tell her of my concerns, although from experience, I am sure she can take care of herself. I slowly move from the tree and walk up the incline, to the dirt path at the top of the hill. I glance left and right as I climb the hill and just as before, no one stands out as a possible foe.

I now have three directions I can go: right toward the bottle and case sales tent; left toward the food and beverage vendors; or straight ahead toward the gift shop. I learned a long time ago to always go with your first thought or direction. I go right toward the tent where they sell wine by the bottle or case and offer wine tasting. I journey past the tent, past the port-a-potties, and turn around when I get to the rear of the main building, which houses the gift shop. Nothing or no one looks suspicious.

I go back to my starting point and head off toward the gift shop. I am now on full-alert mode. I pass by several tables filled with happy customers who are having a great time. I go up on the porch and into the gift shop. People are sampling wine and looking at all of the gifts available to purchase. Still, no one sticks out as a person of interest. I go out the front door and watch as Vicki, from the vineyard, passes by with a medium-sized group, maybe forty people, on a tour of the vineyard. No one seems concerned with me and everyone continues on his or her way.

I go back to my starting point and walk in the direction where vendors are selling sandwiches. The smell wafts into the crowd, drawing hungry folks to try their morsels of delight, while other vendors are selling their favorite beverage. No one is standing out to me. I guess my fears were misguided. Maybe I am getting too old to do this. Maybe Paula Ann was right. I've turned in to a "pops."

All at once I freeze. I spot him, maybe seventy-five yards in front of me, almost hidden by a tree, watching me. Suddenly, my adrenalin goes to high octane and the demons, which up to this point have only been hovering near the surface of my mind, begin to venture out.

He senses I have spotted him and he disappears behind the tree. I don't want to pull my weapon, have somebody yell gun, and start a stampede, so I take off at a brisk walk in his direction. Just past the last vendor, I break into a slow jog and I see him running toward the vineyard area and the parking lot. Just as I am about to start running after him, I notice a black streak come at me from my right side. I am completely surprised by the invasion, catch my foot on a root in the path, and I stumble and fall head over heels on the ground. As I quickly rebound and get up on my hands and knees, I see the villain who attacked me. It is Starr, the vineyard dog, who must have thought I wanted to play with her. She is staring at me with both front legs on the ground, her rear end up in the air and tail wagging. I can tell by the look on her face she is thinking, *well, are you chasing me, or am I chasing you?*

Starr bolts away and as I stand up, I hear a familiar voice behind me. "Mickke D, what the hell are you doing? Are you all right?" Beverly asks.

"Oh, I'm fine. Starr and I were just playing tag. I lost."

Chuck, from the vineyard, and Vicki's *twisted sister* Michelle walk up, followed slowly by Bella, the other vineyard dog. Chuck asks, "Are you OK? I saw you fall. Did Starr trip you?"

"Oh no, she was just playing. Thanks, I'm fine. I was running to catch up with some people I thought I knew and tripped over a root."

Chuck responds, "Darn, I thought I had marked all of those roots with orange paint. Guess I missed that one. Sorry."

Beverly and I pack up and leave fifteen minutes later. My ego and my body are both bruised. Ever since I joined Special Forces in the Army, I considered myself a warrior and that meant to me, once a warrior always a warrior. After today, for the first time in my life, I am starting to doubt that premise and myself.

I don't tell Beverly about the man I had seen and that he was watching me; however, I do get the impression she does not believe the story I told Chuck and Michelle.

The game has now changed. I have seen my adversary. I know what he looks like and it wasn't Larry Meggart. As a matter of fact, he didn't look like any of my four suspects. He was about 5'11, a bald or shaved head, sunglasses and a hip length leather jacket. He almost looked familiar to me. I'll call Detective Concile on Monday morning and give her the news.

ҩ҂ѧ

Once the Hunter gets into his pick-up truck, he starts laughing. Mickke D had fallen flat on his face when that dog ran by him. Maybe he's not as much of an opponent as he once thought. However, there is one new problem. Mickke D has seen his face. He must be a lot more careful from now on.

Chapter 41: The Massage

Sunday morning when I crawl out of bed, I am sore. Monday morning when I get out of bed, I am very sore. I still can't believe I took that tumble on Saturday. My ego has since healed but my body is still bruised. Maybe Paula Ann was right to refer to me as "pops." I have always been much too athletic to stumble and fall like that.

Beverly calls early to check on me and after I tell her how bad I feel, she just laughs and tells me maybe I should go get a massage. The word "massage" brings back some bad vibes.

❧ ❦

My back doctor, Dr. Enloe, several months ago, after a monthly adjustment suggested I get a massage to relieve some of the tension in my neck and shoulders. His assistant Val said she went to a massage parlor and they did a great job. She gave me the name and address. It was located not more than two blocks away so I decided to stop by and check it out on my way home.

The massage parlor was located in a strip shopping center and the sign said open. I walked in and a middle-aged Asian woman walked right up to me and said, "You come on in, we no busy, go in room, take off clothes."

My eyes got big as I replied, "Whoa, I just wanted to check out the price of a massage. My back doctor suggested I try one for the tension in my neck and shoulders."

She never skips a beat. "No problem, regular one-hour, sixty dollar, premium one-hour thirty, seventy-five dollar, you go in room, take of clothes, Debbie be right in." She pointed to a young woman seated in the rear.

Debbie raised her hand and said, "Go in room, take off clothes, I be right in, you like."

Now Debbie may be an American name but this girl was definitely Asian, and may I say, a very lovely and well-put together Asian girl. So, I thought to myself, what the hell, I'm already there, Dr. Enloe prescribed it and Val said they were good.

"Okay, I'll do the regular one-hour massage." I told the woman in charge, whose nametag, I noticed, read Miss Lilly.

The room was actually an area with a massage table in the middle and covered on all sides by draped, colorful sheets. There was a folded white sheet on the table, a chair to one side and a non-descript table close to the entrance. I sat down, took off my shoes and then removed my shirt and pants. I had forgotten that I had put on my bright red silk boxers that day. So there I was standing in bright red boxers and white socks as Debbie walked in. She looked at me, turned to Miss Lilly, said something, which I could not understand, and they both started laughing.

Debbie smiled at me. "You lay on table face down. You sure you no want premium, it better massage."

I said to her with my best puppy dog look. "This is my first massage ever so I think I'll start with the regular one."

"Oh, first time. No problem, I be gentle, you like." She yelled something out to Miss Lilly and they both began laughing again.

I felt her touch my feet as she took off my socks and placed them on the chair with my clothes. I was thinking if she starts to pull off my boxers next, I'm out of there. She took the folded sheet and draped it over the only the part of my body which had something covering it, my butt.

The massage began. She put some kind of oil on my back and began doing her thing. It actually felt pretty good. She then went down to my legs and followed the same procedure. I did get a little nervous when she pushed my boxers up as far as they would go. I made a mental note that if I ever came back to be sure to wear briefs. They would have made me feel a lot more secure at that moment in time. You know, a lot less chance of anything in that area being compromised.

As she had me turn over, I was beginning to feel much more relaxed and began to enjoy her oily hands and elbows all over my body. She was good. She then took hot moist towels. I have no idea where they came from and she wiped off the excess oil from my body. She then proceeded to tell me, "You okay? Now time for hot rocks."

I raised my head up and stammered, "Say what?"

She said, "No problem, you like, feel good."

She then applied more oil and proceeded to take some sort of a flat smooth stone, which was very warm, to the point of being hot, and rubbed them all over my body. I was fine until she got down right close to some very sensitive parts of my anatomy. In addition, those rocks were very hot. They could have done some real damage; however, I persevered and made it through the ordeal.

Finally, my hour was up and again, the hot moist towels appeared out of nowhere and she wiped me down again. Before she said I was finished she asked again, "You sure you don't want premium, only fifteen dollar for thirty more?"

Since I had no idea what the premium consisted of and probably didn't want to know, I told her I was fine, maybe next time. I paid Miss Lilly and left Debbie a tip.

ॐॐ

Therefore, when Beverly suggests I go have a massage, I tell her, "I don't think so. Maybe I'll just let you give me a massage."

She replies, "Yeah, right," and abruptly ends our conversation.

Chapter 42: The Office

On my way to the office, I keep thinking I have seen the man at La Belle Amie Vineyard somewhere before. Then it hits me. He could be the same person I saw in that fuzzy video from the Tricia Lynn Motel or the person from the boat on the waterway.

I hobble into the office around 10 a.m. and I can tell by the atmosphere that Beverly has spread the word about my non-warrior type performance on Saturday.

Jim sticks his head out of his office and laughingly says, "Say boss, you want to race? I'll give you a head start but watch out for those roots. They'll get you every time."

"Very funny," I reply as I give Beverly a sarcastic look.

She just smiles and curtly says, "Maybe Jim will give you a massage."

As I start down the hallway, I notice there is a light on in Mark's office so I figure I have one more dig coming before I make it to the safe confines of my office. I was right. "Hey boss, I hear you've been practicing your crash and roll from jump school?"

I return his volley with, "Hey Yale, don't you have a tree to plant somewhere?"

I go in my office and close the door. To my surprise and amazement, on the rear side of the door is a photocopy of me on all fours, looking at Starr. I'm guessing Beverly took it with her cell phone. I rip the picture off the door and as I toss it into the wastebasket my phone rings. It's Beverly and she's laughing along with Jim and Mark. "Don't worry, we have the negative," they reply in unison.

"Very funny and by the way, does anyone work in this office?" The laughter stops and the phone goes dead.

As I'm contemplating calling Detective Concile, I have a flash back of Saturday. How did Beverly get there so quickly to take that photo? Was she following me and if so, why? She always seems to be around when trouble breaks out.

I sit down at my desk and put a call into Detective Concile. I'm hoping she has a sketch artist in her office. I still think my guy and the guy at the Tricia Lynn could be one in the same. Her phone goes to voicemail and I leave her a message that I need to speak with her ASAP. Within thirty seconds, she returns my call.

She starts the conversation with, "Mickke D, if someone else is missing, I don't want to hear about it."

"No one new is missing that I know of, however, I am almost certain that I saw our serial killer on Saturday at La Belle Amie Vineyard."

Silence fills the air space between our phones. Finally, she says, "Really. What makes you think it was our killer?"

I fill her in with my Saturday encounter but leave out the part where I stumble and fall. I tell her he eluded me at the last minute. Then I ask, "Do you have a sketch artist available? I think I have seen this guy before."

"Sure, when can you come in and give him a description?"

"I'll be there in about thirty minutes."

As I leave the office, I get my own dig in as I say loudly for all to hear. "I hope everyone in this office has more to do than ridicule their boss. You know, the guy who signs their checks and passes out Christmas bonuses."

There is no comment from Jim or Mark. Beverly waves good-bye and is trying very hard not to laugh.

☜☞

I arrive at the police station and within forty-five minutes, the sketch artist has produced an excellent drawing of our suspect.

I call Detective Concile over to the sketch artist desk. "That's him. That's the guy at the vineyard on Saturday and I think he is the same guy from the Tricia Lynn video and the same guy who tried to crash into us on the waterway."

She signals for me to follow her. "Come into my office, let's talk about this."

I enter her office and take a seat in front of her desk as she closes her door. "So detective, are you going to put the drawing out to the public?"

"Well, I'm not sure. If we take it to the public, he will know that we know what he looks like and he may go underground. If we just put it out to law enforcement, he may think you did not get a good look at him and maybe he'll stay visible."

"But if you don't put it out to the public and he kills again, what then?"

"That's my dilemma, Mickke D, not yours. My question to you is what makes you so sure he is our killer? That video from the motel is very fuzzy and it's hard to make out that man's face. He had a hat on, and you said the guy on the waterway had on a poncho."

"To me it's very simple, he was watching, hiding, and he ran. Even if it's not him, the guy that ran was up to no good and if you arrest him, you can find out who he is and if he has a record."

She ponders my statement. "Okay Mickke D, thanks for your help. I'll let you know what I decide to do."

After Mickke D leaves her office, she weighs the pros and cons of her next move. About thirty minutes later, she makes her decision.

Chapter 43: Stephanie

More and more days pass without any real treasure being found on the sunken pirate ship, the Queen Beth, off the Coast of Pawleys Island. The recovery team is finding relics from the ship, including cannons, cannon balls, and an occasional spattering of coins, which of course are going to be worth a lot of money. However, each day that goes by without finding gold, silver, and jewels is a welcome ending of the day for TC. The latest discovery by his team was several large rotting chests filled with nothing but rocks and stones, but nothing of real value. To him, this means the logbook is correct. Captain Swinely did bury his plunder somewhere on shore.

Stephanie Langchester is also concerned that no treasure has been found. She had researched the ship with friends back in England and from what they discovered, the Queen Beth should have been full of ill-gotten gains.

She is still wondering what TC found that day outside the ship. He has been a completely different person since that day. He spends less time underwater and more time going over the large cache of maps he keeps locked up on his boat. When she asks him about the maps, he just says he is working on his next salvage venture.

Stephanie needs to get a look at those maps and maybe see if she can find out what he found on the ocean floor that day.

She knows TC's schedule like the back of her hand. They all meet at the Crazy Sister's Marina in Murrells Inlet each morning, weather permitting, at 7 a.m. except Saturday and Sunday. They board TC's boat and go out to the salvage ship, which stays anchored above the Queen Beth's location. There are two guards, hired by the State of South Carolina, on the salvage vessel from 6 in the evening until TC picks them up when he drops off the girls the next morning. There are guards there 24/7 on Saturday and Sunday. The guards are there as a deterrent against any claim jumpers trying to get in on the action. As the girls are getting ready for the day ahead, TC shuttles the guards back to the marina. He returns and the girls go to work. TC supervises at the underwater site and from the salvage vessel. At the end of the day, they transfer whatever small to medium items they have salvaged on TC's boat and take it along with the girls back to the mainland. Once on dry land, TC shuttles the two guards back out to the salvage ship while the girls take their findings and put them into a warehouse with large saltwater vats for processing on Saturday. Friday evenings the salvage ship brings in the larger items and unloads them at the marina. TC stays on site until the salvage ship returns. On Saturday and Sunday, TC shuttles the guards back and forth and then on Saturday they photograph each item, write a description, and categorize it.

Stephanie devises a plan to get on TC's boat without him being around. The team of girls, plus TC, usually starts around 9 in the morning on Saturday and spend about four hours doing what they refer to as paperwork. Stephanie tells TC on Friday that she has a dental appointment on Saturday morning and that she won't be at the warehouse until late morning.

She arrives at the marina around 8:30 and goes directly to TC's boat. She knows that he has made his run with the guards and usually gets back to the marina around 8. The compartment where he keeps the maps is locked; picking the lock is not a problem for her. She retrieves the maps and places them on a table. After unrolling them and looking them over, she quickly decides TC is looking for treasure on land not on the ocean floor. She finds three maps with X's marked on them and she takes photos of those maps along with all of the other maps, with her iPhone camera. She thinks to herself, *if only Queue could have put together one of these for James Bond.* She looks around the boat to see if she can find whatever it was that TC found that day in the ocean, but comes up empty. So the question is, do the maps have anything to do with whatever it was TC found on the ocean floor or is this just as he stated, a completely different and new venture?

She places everything back where it was on the boat and arrives at the warehouse around 10 where she discovers that while TC and the team were going through the remains of the rotting chests and the rubble of rocks and stones, they found a solitary gold ring. TC brushes it off as just the fact that someone had lost a ring, but he knows this is the final chapter in his story. The loot is somewhere on land. Stephanie is beginning to think the same thing. The reason she did not find the logbook on the boat is because TC keeps it at home in his bedroom wall safe, and thanks to TC, Stephanie and her team will soon know exactly where it is located.

Chapter 44: The Dinner Party

It has been almost two weeks since my last encounter with my suspected killer. Sam decided not to put the sketch out to the public, only to law enforcement, and so far so good, no new missing persons and no one has died that we know of. However, her investigation into the murder of Jennifer Holmes, Ray Bonsai, and the other missing persons is going nowhere fast. The police have interviewed quite a few people, including my suspects, but they still have nothing to go on.

Around 3 on Wednesday afternoon, I get a call from TC. "Hey Mickke D, have you found your serial killer yet?"

"No TC, things have been quiet on that subject. What's going on?"

"Well, I'm having a small get-together on Saturday night at my house for the girls on the salvage team. They have been working hard and besides that, they keep asking about you. Thought you might like to come down and bring Beverly with you. It will be a chance for you to meet the girls and thank them for their help. Also, I would like to talk to you about the maps."

"Sure TC, count us in. I would like to meet your motley crew and if I bring Beverly along, hopefully I'll stay out of trouble. Do we need to bring anything?"

"No, just yourselves. I'll take care of the rest."

I call Beverly. This is her day off and Jannie, Mark's wife, is covering the phones in the office today. Beverly finally answers her phone and sounds out of breath. "Hey Mickke D, what's up?"

"Just wanted to know if you have any plans for Saturday night? TC invited us down to his place for dinner. He is inviting his salvage crew, you know the four girls from England I told you about. Might be fun."

"Sounds like a plan, call me with a time, got to run, see ya."

That was strange. I didn't even get a chance to ask her what she was doing and why she sounded out of breath. Maybe she was taking one of her infamous self-defense classes.

ை∽

I drive the Corvette to TC's and Beverly does not slam the door this time. We arrive at his home at the Heritage Plantation on Pawleys Island around 6 p.m. The girls and TC are all sitting out around the pool, a huge area completely enclosed with glass and screens. As I walk down the three steps to the pool area, I remember the first time I was here and the lovely, bikini clad twins who were sitting by the pool that day. I wonder where they are today.

The moment I ask the question, I know I should have kept my mouth shut. "TC, what happened to the twins who used to take care of your pool?"

Stephanine jumps right in. "Yes, TC, tell us about the twins?"

Beverly can't resist. "Yes, TC, tell us about the twins that Mickke D remembers so well."

TC looks my way. "The last I heard they were in Virginia Beach."

TC changes the subject and quickly makes the introductions. He hands Beverly a glass of Chardonnay and me a beer. Besides Stephanie, there is Pat Livingrock, an auburn-haired English tart who has a handshake almost as strong as my ex-commanding officer at Fort Bragg. Jenny Blare has strawberry blond hair and a cute smile. Karen Bruogg could almost be Stephanie's sister but much shorter. All four of the girls are probably in their mid-thirties to early forties and supposedly single. They all give me a thorough once over.

TC was right, the girls are stunning, almost too stunning. And he was right about Stephanie being a knockout. However, my investigative mind quickly gets in the way and overrides other parts of my body. I look past the beauty and gaze at her eyes. They are like ice. This woman has been around the block a few times. She is a pro. Her mind and body are in complete control of the situation. You can tell right away that she is the boss. I can also tell she is sizing me up as well.

I am watching Beverly's reaction to the initial meeting with the girls. I can tell she too senses something different about these women. From the look on her face, I deduce she is sizing up the entire bunch and trying to decide how to handle the situation. This could prove to be a very interesting evening.

TC has Bistro 217 cater his dinner. The dinner begins with a pear salad followed by Southern fish and chips and shrimp and grits, along with sides of potato salad and fried green tomatoes. Dessert is pecan pie. Everything is delicious.

After dinner, we are sitting around the pool and making small talk. I notice one strange thing. The girls are still sipping on their original drink they had when we walked in. I'm on my second beer and Beverly is on her second glass of wine. TC has offered to refill their glasses but they all refused. Now one of them, Pat, asks TC where the powder room is and he points her in the right direction. She nonchalantly looks at all three of the other girls and leaves. For some reason, I check my watch.

The small talk resumes and when Pat returns she whispers something to Karen, who also excuses herself. I check my watch again and notice Pat was gone for almost ten minutes. That seems like a long time to just pee.

Karen returns and whispers in Jenny's ear and she leaves. Again, Jenny is gone for almost ten minutes. The same thing happens with Stephanie. Between the four girls, they spend almost forty minutes in the powder room. If I didn't know better, I just might think they are casing TC's house.

Beverly gets up and asks the way to the powder room and the girls tell her the way. She returns in three minutes. Something strange is going on here. Now it's my turn. "Well, since everyone else is going to the bathroom, I guess I will also."

This produces a small laugh from the four girls; however, Beverly and TC just stare at me with a strange look on their faces. TC gives me directions. I walk back through the tiled kitchen and great room. The bathroom is just off the great room in a hallway which leads to what I suppose are bedrooms. The hallway is carpeted with a heavy wool carpet, which I can tell has been vacuumed lately. I can see footprints going into the bathroom and more footprints going down the hallway and into each of the three bedrooms. The footprints are small, like that of a woman. Someone has been looking around.

I return to the pool area just as Stephanie asks TC to give them a tour of the house. Within seconds, we are all following TC on a sightseeing trip through his gorgeous home. I decide to bring up the rear, which I can tell does not sit well with Stephanie. She does not like the idea of someone behind her. The girls are very attentive to TC's description of each room and quite the perfect guests, commenting on how beautiful everything is. They are particularly enchanted with the huge master bedroom and spend a lot of time looking around after TC and Beverly have moved on to the next room. As I stick my head into the master bedroom, Stephanie has her finger up to her mouth, as if to say, *don't say a word, he's still in the hallway.*

I can't for the life of me figure out what they are looking for, but they are definitely looking for something. I have learned that being suspicious can be a healthy affliction, one that just may prolong your life. I continue on without them.

We finish our trip around the house and TC suggest that all the girls play pool, in the swimming pool area while he and I go over some business, then we'll all have that pecan pie for dessert. I'm thinking, *"should I leave Beverly alone with those girls? This could get ugly."*

TC and I go into his office, close the door, and he pulls out the cache of maps. Before we get started, I ask him, "Is there anything in this house that your girls would want to steal from you?"

TC has a baffled look on his face. "What are you talking about? Why would they want to steal anything?"

"Let me ask you this. Do you have a wall safe somewhere in the house?"

"Yes, in the master bedroom."

"Do you have anything of value in it?"

He thinks for a second or two before answering. "Not really, just some cash and I do keep the old logbook from the Queen Beth there. Why do you ask?

"Oh, I guess I'm just thinking out loud. Tell me what you found on the maps."

"Okay Mickke D, let me tell you what I have discovered since I began researching the maps we received from your friend Susan."

"TC, she's an acquaintance, not a friend."

"By the way, I had a very nice evening with Susan and Bess after you left. Bess asked several times if you were in a relationship and of course, I replied that you were."

"Great, now just continue with your story." I had pretty much forgotten about Susan until TC had to go and mention her name.

He continues. "So, anyway, my first guess of where the treasure was buried was of course, the area around Georgetown. However, here's what I found out. The Georgetown area was the probable site of the first European settlement in North America in 1526 but the community did not last long. Georgetown itself was not founded until 1729 and became a port of entry in 1732. Before then, all foreign exports and imports had to pass through Charles Town, which is Charleston today. Duties and added freight had to be paid there. With the designation of Georgetown as a port of entry, the area's merchants and planters could deal directly with all ports, bypassing Charleston and the designation brought added business to the town."

"And what does that have to do with the map?" I ask.

"Well, first of all, let me tell you about the pirates during that period in time."

"Great, but see if you can work the map in somehow," I plead.

He went on to tell me that during the early 1700s pirates flourished, particularly in the area we now know as Charleston. Many colonial merchants traded with pirates so as not to have to pay taxes to the King of England. However, after pirates began capturing ships carrying commercial cargo belonging to wealthy men in the Charleston area, they decided to end the pirate trade. Pirates soon became a menace to the local population throughout Charleston and along the Carolina coast.

Most of the pirates during that time were based out of the Bahamas and they would sail to the South Carolina coast to capture ships sailing into the area. Some of the more infamous pirates were "Gentleman Pirate" Stede Bonnet, who left Barbados to seek adventure on the high seas, along with Edward Teach, better known as Blackbeard. Also there was Anne Bonny, one of the more famous female pirates of the time, and Calico Jack Rackham, best known for his fancy calico attire.

Piracy was also influential in the naming of several locations along the South Carolina coast. Drunken Jack Island supposedly was named for a pirate who drank too much and died on the island, while Murrells Inlet was allegedly named after Captain John Murrell, who used the inlet as a base to prey on ships at sea.

Then in 1718, the governor of South Carolina launched a huge attempt to find and destroy pirates. Several ships were sunk during that period of time. Piracy pretty much died out after 1722, which was seven years before Georgetown was founded. Therefore, if the date in the logbook is correct, the Queen Beth was sunk thirteen years prior to the founding of Georgetown. Then the question is, would there have been a town or even buildings there at that time?

"Well TC, if it wasn't buried around Georgetown, then where was it buried? And are you really sure it was buried at all?"

He goes on to tell me about the gold ring he found in the chest full of rotting canvas and rocks, along with the fact that they have found nothing of real value on the Queen Beth except the coins. TC really believes the treasure was buried so I guess I'm a believer also, at least for the time being.

෧ං෪

After Mickke D moves on down the hallway, Stephanie thinks she spots what she has been trying to find in the master bedroom. All of the pictures hanging on TC's walls are off by a little bit. After running her finger over the top of each piece of artwork, she can tell they have been recently cleaned and dusted. Whoever did the housecleaning did not adjust them back to level or else they just had a bad eye for what is level, because now they are not perfectly level. Only someone with a trained eye would have noticed. Only one painting, located on an inside wall next to his closet, is level. They enter the huge walk-in closet during the tour and all of the girls comment on how big it is. Stephanie notices that the wall behind the painting has only one low rack for hanging clothes. The upper part of the wall is comprised of drawers and small storage areas with lockable doors. She thinks one or more of those doors is a fake, and that it will not open even with a key. She saw a similar set up in Monte Carlo several years ago. She believes this is where his safe is located and that the painting is attached to the wall with concealable hinges so therefore it will stay level.

She pulls on one side of the painting and it doesn't budge. She then tries the other side and just like magic, it swings open and reveals a flush wall safe. She takes several pictures of the safe with her phone. One of the things she took with her when she left British Intelligence was a thumb drive with pictures and descriptions of probably every wall safe manufactured in the world, with descriptions and instructions for getting inside. She just knew that it would come in handy someday and that day may be very close.

෧ං෪

While Mickke D and TC are doing whatever it is that they are doing, Stephanie has plans of her own and it's not playing pool. She tells Jenny to distract Beverly by taking her outside to see Mickke D's Corvette. While they are away, she takes photos with her cell phone of all the doors and windows in this part of the house, including the sliding glass door from the pool area into the main house. She notices that there is no locking rod to help secure the sliding glass door from opening when locked. She also goes searching for an alarm system, which she can't seem to find. She finishes her surveillance just as Jenny and Beverly return. The girls and Beverly begin playing pea pool and Beverly cleans their clock.

Stephanie doesn't want to, but she has to ask, "TC, I'll bet you have an elaborate alarm system to keep this beautiful house safe. How much did it cost?"

"Nothing, I just keep the doors and windows locked. There's really nothing of value anyone can steal and I've had some bad experiences with alarm systems in the past."

Stephanie grins. "Well, I guess that makes sense. If you don't need it, why have it?"

I don't say anything but I'm wondering to myself, why would she ask that question? But then again, maybe I'm just over analyzing the situation.

Chapter 45: The Cartel

It's around 8:15 Tuesday morning and I am leaving the house for my monthly chiropractor's appointment with Dr. Enloe in Myrtle Beach. As I pass the Little River Bowling Lanes, which is located just outside of River Hills, I notice an older, black SUV sitting alone in the parking lot. I'm not sure why it caught my eye, maybe because all of the windows seemed to be tinted black. It has an eerie, up-to-no-good look to it.

I turn right out of River Hills and while passing Collision Masters and Sunny Side Up, I happen to check my right side passenger door mirror and I notice the black SUV pull out and turn right onto 17. My pulse quickens.

I continue down 17 and get off on Route 9 heading toward Loris. As I pass the old, now closed, Bay Tree golf courses, the fairways and greens now cluttered with tall weeds instead of golf carts filled with golfers, I check my rear-view mirror and the black SUV is just merging onto Route 9. I tell myself there is no reason to get excited, at least not yet. I can't think of anyone who would want to tail me except for maybe Detective Concile; however, her people would have a much newer vehicle and after their last debacle while tailing me, they probably would have been more secretive and less visible. Maybe this is who I have felt was watching me all this time.

I opt to find out if I really do have a pursuer, so I pull into the Food Lion parking lot, drive through, and park on the far side close to my dentist's office. I watch in my rear-view mirror as the black SUV turns right at the light but instead of continuing toward the Food Lion he stops and parks at the O'Reilly's Auto Parts Store. Two men get out of the car. See there, I was getting worried for no reason at all. I leave the parking lot, get back onto Route 9 and then get on Highway 31 South. I turn up the volume on my favorite radio station 105.9 and continue my trip to Dr. Enloe's office.

As I pass the exit for the Main Street Connector, my pulse quickens again. I'm in the far right lane and I spot the black SUV traveling behind me in the middle lane. I have the cruise set on 70 and the black SUV is located about seventy-five yards behind me, off to my left and not gaining. There is no way those two guys could have gone into that store and come out again that quickly to be this close to me. There is very little traffic on Highway 31, so I am having no problem keeping the SUV in view. If it's not Detective Concile, then it must be a more dangerous adversary. I can only think of two, the guy who has been stalking me and trying to kill me or the Colombian drug cartel. Since there are two men in the car, I'm guessing it's the latter.

More than fifteen years ago, I was heading up a Special Forces special ops team in Colombia to find and destroy the drug trade. We were in country disguised strictly as a training team for the Colombian Army with no offensive desires or capabilities. A bounty was put on my head after we found and destroyed millions of dollars of cocaine before it could be shipped out of the country. The army transferred me to Panama after several threats and assassination attempts.

I had pretty much forgotten about that chapter of my life until about eight months ago when an assassin from Colombia tried to kill me at my home. I guess that bounty may still be in effect. He did not succeed, and now, if I'm right, here we go again. I can feel my old demons beginning to emerge as we approach the turnoff to Highway 22 and Conway.

I opt to see if my thoughts are true or just nervous, unrealistic falsehoods. I signal that I am going to get off on Highway 22. At the last second, I veer left and get back on Highway 31. I learned that maneuver from watching tourists do that same move during the summer months. My adversary also moves into the right lane to exit and then swerves back onto Highway 31. I now can safely say the black SUV is the enemy so now it boils down to one thing, self-preservation. It's them or me.

The demons are filling my body with adrenalin and I will do whatever it takes to eliminate the enemy. I stare out the windshield and I see myself back in the jungles of Colombia. I am dressed in camouflaged fatigues, a floppy hat, and camouflage covers my face. The people in that black SUV have no idea who they are dealing with.

I retrieve my .45 from the storage compartment between the front bucket seats and with my knees guiding my vehicle; I pull the slide, arm the weapon, and place it on the passenger seat. I check to make sure my seatbelt is tight and locked. I open my cell phone and dial 911.

A very relaxed and quiet voice answers my call. "This is the 911 operator, what is your emergency?"

"My name is Mickke MacCandlish and I need you to send the patrol and an ambulance to Highway 31. I'm going south in a white Chevy Trailblazer on 31 between 22 and Robert Grissom Parkway."

"Has there been an accident and is anyone injured?" her tone of her voice does not change.

"Not yet ma'am, but it won't be long." I close my phone, place it in the middle compartment and close the lid. I hit the down button and lower my side window.

The first shot shatters my back window and the right side rear window. The second shot gets my left rear window, my rear-view mirror and the windshield. That one was close. I feel the heat from the bullet as it barely misses my right ear. I need to do something immediately. I can't fire backwards and hit anything. You only see that in the movies. With both feet, I hit the brake pedal hard. The sound of screaming tires and burning rubber fill the inside of my vehicle. I am guessing the brakes on the older SUV are nowhere close to being as good as my brakes, so maybe my plan will work. As I am sliding, the black SUV cannot stop as quickly so all of a sudden he catches up and is right beside me with tires screeching. With one hand on the steering wheel, and both feet on the brake, I clamp my right hand on my weapon and deposit three rounds into the passenger side window and a fourth shot into the right front tire. The other driver loses control and slams into my SUV. My last thought is that of a sensation of rolling over, and over, and over, the sound of crushing metal and then complete silence.

I see images of myself floating above a large hammock strung between two large palm trees. There is a phone attached to one of the trees and it is ringing. I answer and it's Val from Dr. Enloe's office. She wants to know why I did not show up for my appointment Tuesday morning. Then there is a feeling of falling and then nothing. Blackness covers my world.

Chapter 46: The Break-In

Stephanie needs to get into TC's house and have a look in the wall safe. She opts to take Karen with her. She needs to have someone watch her back, and be a lookout for any unanticipated trouble. While at TC's party, she noticed a copy of the Property Owners Association Directory. She leafed through it and mentally wrote down a couple of the names. When she made her bathroom trip, she physically wrote them in her notebook.

The Heritage Plantation is a gated community. During daylight hours, if you just tell the security guard you are going to the golf course, you will have no problem. Stephanie knows TC goes to the gym every Monday, Wednesday, and Friday evening from 7 until 8 p.m. They will have one hour to do their thing. For that time period, they can't use the golf course as a means of entry. Also, TC told them there is a roving security guard on duty from 6 at night until 6 in the morning. That was another reason he felt as if he did not need an alarm system.

They arrive at the security gate around 6:30. They have on wigs and large glasses which hide their true features. They tell the guard they are meeting Anne Kippen for dinner at the club. He replies, "Oh, she is such a lovely woman. Have you ever heard her sing?"

Stephanie looks at Karen and then answers, "No we haven't."

"Well, you should hear her sing sometime, she has a beautiful voice. Someone told me she sang with a famous band back in the day. Can't remember the name of the band, but anyway, you ladies enjoy your dinner." He hands Stephanie a pass and tells her to drop it in the return box on the way out.

They have made it over the first hurdle, but just barely. They hang the visitor pass on their rear-view mirror and proceed through the gate. TC's house is only two blocks from the clubhouse, so they park the car in the parking lot and take off the wigs and glasses. They push their hair up and under a ball cap, take off their jackets, and reveal warm-up pants and sweat shirts. Stephanie has everything she needs in her attached fanny pack, including a small .25 caliber gun. They begin walking in the direction of TC's house. Stephanie checks her watch. It is 6:43 and getting dark outside.

When they get to within two houses of TC's house, they stop. TC is just pulling out of his circular driveway. He turns and goes in the opposite direction of where they are standing. The girls take a deep breath and speed up their walk until they get right in front of the house. They look around, see no one and walk quickly around to the back of the house. They are now out of view from the main street.

They walk up to the screen door leading into the pool area and both of them are startled when an outside security light comes on. Stephanie quickly jiggles the hooked latch with a thin, small, metal ruler, and they are in the pool area. Within a few seconds, the outside light goes out. Stephanie looks at Karen and says, "Remember that light when we leave."

Karen is not used to breaking into homes. Her mouth is dry as a bone but she does manage to answer. "No problem. I need a drink of water."

Stephanie scolds her, "You can have a drink of water when we get back to the condo. Don't touch anything in here, don't turn on any lights, just watch the back yard. If you see anyone, whistle just as we practiced. I won't be long."

Stephanie removes her shoes, leaves the pool area, turns on her pocket pen light and goes straight to the sliding glass door. She easily picks the lock, opens the door and goes directly to the master bedroom. She had looked up the wall safe on her thumb drive. The safe is constructed of heavy gauge steel with a digital keypad. It has three steel locking bolts and a power override box. It fits between 16-inch wall studs and has an unusually deep box, probably eighteen inches. It most likely cost between $350 and $500.

She reaches into her fanny pack and pulls out a small black battery operated box with a digital read out screen. She connects a small probe to the box, which has a small suction cup on the other end. She then attaches the suction cup to the digital keypad on the front of the safe. She turns on the black box and numbers start flashing across the screen. In less than a minute, a six-digit number appears. She releases the suction cup, turns off the black box and presses the six numbers on the keypad. A bell softly rings; she hears a click and the door pops open. She looks in the safe and sees papers, some cash, and something in a zip lock plastic container. She takes out the container, opens it and pulls out what looks like an old book. It has a musty smell to it. She opens the book and quickly realizes it is an old ship's logbook. She leafs through the book and finds the map. She immediately takes a picture with her cell phone of the map along with a few of the handwritten pages including the pages where she found the map. She smiles. *So this is what he found, a treasure map. Now everything is beginning to make sense.*

She checks her watch. It is 7:18, time to leave. She places the book back in the container and back into the safe just as she found it. She closes the door to the safe. She quickly returns to the pool area where Karen is anxiously waiting her return. Next, she relocks the sliding door by pushing a button on the inside and as she closes the door, it locks. As she and Karen leave, they are again startled by the security light. They slowly walk around the side of the house and look all around before going out to the street. They walk back to the parking lot, change back into wigs and glasses, and leave the plantation.

Just as they are passing the security gate, a car is coming into the plantation. The guard is pre-occupied with that incoming vehicle. They quickly drop the pass into the return box. The guard says to the occupant, "Good evening Mrs. Kippen. Your dinner guests arrived almost forty-five minutes ago."

Anne Kippen gets a puzzled look on her face. "What dinner guest? I'm not meeting any dinner guests."

The gate guard waves her through and gets on his radio. He calls the roving security guard. He gives the guard a vague description of Stephanie's vehicle and the two women inside. He tells him to search for the SUV and the two women but the girls are already gone.

⊱⊰

TC arrives home about 8:20. He goes directly to the kitchen for a drink of water. He is a rather meticulous type of person; he wants a place for everything and everything in the proper place. He has a towel on the counter beside the sink where he places his glass after having a drink of water and rinsing the glass. He always sets the glass in the left-hand corner, just off the edge of the towel so that air can get inside the glass and dry it. The glass is in the left-hand corner; however, it is at least one inch from the edge of the towel. He would never do that. He picks up the glass, turns it over and it is still wet inside. He then looks at the kitchen faucet. When he is finished using the faucet, he always places it directly over the middle of the double sink. The faucet is over the left-hand sink. Someone has been in his house.

After spending time with Mickke D, he now keeps two loaded guns in the house, one in a drawer beside his bed and one in the kitchen, under his kitchen towels. He reaches under the towels and retrieves the weapon. He goes out to the sliding glass door, which opens into the pool area. The door is locked. He turns on all the lights in the pool area, unlocks the door and ventures forward, gun in hand. He walks around the pool and over to the screen door leading outside. The screen door is not latched. He remembers being outside in the yard prior to leaving for the gym. He is positive he remembers setting the hook when he came back inside. He latches the door.

As he is leaving the pool area, a terrible thought crosses his mind. He quickly moves to the master bedroom and goes up to the picture covering his wall safe and pulls back the frame.

The wall safe is closed. He opens the safe and breathes a sigh of relief. The logbook and map are there. He counts the cash and nothing is missing. He checks all of the remaining rooms in the house and returns to the kitchen, puts his weapon back under the towels and turns off the lights to the pool area. He goes into his office and turns on his computer. There is a blinking yellow alert from the Security Division in the development to be on the lookout for a green Chevy Tahoe or maybe a Suburban with two women inside. The message contains nothing specific. It is only an alert. Stephanie and the girls drive a green Chevy Tahoe, but then again, so do thousands of other people.

Just in case, he decides it is time to take some precautions.

বঙ্গ

When Stephanie and Karen return to the condo, they, along with Jenny and Pat, have a meeting about what they plan to do next. Stephanie shows everyone the picture of the map. She receives mixed reactions from her crew. Jenny starts out by saying, "What do we know about finding buried treasure on land? Where would we start?"

Pat says, "I think it would be great, but like Jenny said, where would we begin, and do we have the time? We work ten hours a day the way it is."

Stephanie then looks at Karen. "And Karen, what do you think? And by the way, did you get your drink of water?"

Karen gets a bewildered look on her face. "I'll go along with whatever the rest of you want to do. And yes, Steph. I got my drink of water."

Stephanie suddenly stands up and looks directly at Karen. "Did we re-hook the screen door?"

"I certainly didn't. I wouldn't know how to begin. I thought you did."

Stephanie places both hands on her head. "It was that damn security light! Maybe he'll just think he forgot to hook it."

The girls all look at each other and then Karen finally says, "Does that mean we are going to be arrested?"

Stephanie immediately replies, "Of course not, there's no way of ever proving we were in his house. No one saw us, and we left no fingerprints or any evidence of our being there, did we Karen?"

Karen, trying to sound as believable as possible, says, "Not from me."

Stephanie is beginning to think her plan is beginning to fall apart. She and the girls have been working long hours and the tension is beginning to turn in to stress. She can feel it in the room, like a thick fog enveloping everyone. "Okay, for now we'll stick with the original plan. Everyone get a good night's sleep."

Stephanie goes into her bedroom and gets out her notebook. She turns on her computer and loads the photo of the map. She then makes a copy, folds it, and places it in the notebook. She deletes the picture from her phone. She goes to the back of the notebook and looks at the page where she estimates how much they have found on the Queen Beth and what it may be worth. So far, she estimates they have found gold and silver coins worth around two million dollars and the remainder of the salvage items could go for another two million. That's a total of four million; however, after you pay a third party fifty percent to fence the loot for you, and then split the remainder four ways, that's not much for all of their time and effort.

Stephanie decides it may be time for plan B. Only she knows what plan B is.

Chapter 47: The Hospital

More strange images. Blue and I are in this huge bowl filled with potato chips and caramel corn. Blue is content with just eating everything in sight but for some reason I continue to try to get out of the bowl. I keep sliding back down the edge of the bowl but I try again, and again, I slide back down. I finally get a grip on the edge of the bowl.

I open my eyes slowly. The bright lights are glaring and it takes a while for my eyes to adjust. Where am I? I can feel that my head is bandaged and I have several plastic tubes running out of different parts of my body. I must be in a hospital, but why? I look around and see no one in the room. I hear a "dinging" noise and then a nurse enters the room.

"Hello Mr. MacCandlish, I'm your nurse, nice to see you've come around to join us."

I look around the room to see if there is anyone else in the room because I don't know any Mr. MacCandlish. I try to say something but my mouth doesn't want to form the words. With great difficulty, I finally ask a slurred question. "You look familiar, do I know you?"

She looks at me and says, "I don't think so. My name is Bonnie Somerset."

I lose my grip on the edge of the bowl and fall down to the bottom. Darkness arrives again.

❧❦

I can't understand why someone doesn't put a ladder in this damn big bowl. It would make it so much easier to get out. As I open my eyes this time, there are two other people in the room and neither one of them is dressed like a nurse. One is a lovely young woman who I would love to have as a nurse. The other is an older guy wearing glasses and sporting a big smile.

I guess they didn't notice I had opened my eyes so I say with great difficulty, "Who are you and is anyone taking care of Blue?" Then, I think to myself, "*who is Blue?*"

The young lady answers, "Mickke D, remember us? Beverly and Jim. How are you feeling?"

"Beverly and Jim who? And no, I don't feel well, I have a tremendous headache. And what did you call me, Mickke D? Who would name their child Mickke D?"

Jim comes back with, "Yes, that's your name and you should see the other guys."

The woman who is calling herself Beverly frowns at him and says, "Knock it off Jim, wait until he at least knows who he is."

The door opens and nurse Bonnie is back. She is followed into the room by a lady dressed in a white coat. She introduces herself, "Mickke D, its Dr. Mount. Remember me?"

"Not really doc, should I?"

"Bonnie, I think we should clear the room and let Mr. Mac-Candlish rest for a while. I think he's still in la-la land."

After everyone leaves, Dr. Mount says to me, "Mickke D, you have a bad concussion, but other than that, you're not that bad off. You should be able to leave in a couple of days. Nothing seems to be broken so you will just have to take it easy for a while." Once again, I fall back into that huge green bowl.

⊱⊰

Two days later, I finally get out of my big green bowl. I wake-up and I feel as if I had only been asleep for eight hours. The truth be known, I was out for about four days. Instead of Beverly and Jim sitting in my room, this time there is a new person, my old friend Detective Concile along with Dr. Mount and my nurse. Dr. Mount called Detective Concile when I seemed about to wake up with no problems. Nurse Bonnie hands me a glass of water and leaves the room.

Sam jumps on my case right away. "Mickke D, why do I only see you after you have gotten yourself into some sort of trouble?"

I jab right back. "Yes detective, I'm fine, thank you for asking and as usual it was self-defense on my part, and I do remember calling 911 to let them know there was going to be a problem."

She almost smiles but at the last minute holds back. "Yes, you did, and then you proceeded to cause a major accident on 31 by shooting up an SUV next to you."

"By the way, what happened to the two guys in the other vehicle and were they from Colombia?"

"They were dead when the emergency vehicles got to them and yes, they were from Colombia. We found fake ID cards and passports in their vehicle. Someone down there doesn't like you Mickke D."

I then ask, "What about my Trailblazer?"

"It's totaled. You were lucky to get away with only a bad concussion."

Just then, Beverly and Jim enter my room and Jim says, "Hey boss, you're looking much better this time."

Beverly comes over and kisses my cheek. "Do you know who we are this time?"

"What do you mean by that? I've always known who you guys are."

Jim laughs, "Yeah, right."

Detective Concile leaves but reminds me on her way out the door that I need to come down to the station and fill out a report about the accident and shooting. Beverly and Jim pack me up and take me home. Blue seems happy to see me but I think Beverly spoiled him because he is really hanging around her.

After they leave, I call my insurance company and they steer me to a rental company for a car while awaiting word from them about a new vehicle. While I am waiting for the car to arrive, I begin to think about what I am going to do about my Colombian problem.

Chapter 48: Colonel Townsend

I decide it's time to do something about my Colombian dilemma. I don't want to spend the rest of my life continually looking over my shoulder to see if someone is following me or watching me.

I put a call into Colonel Townsend, my ex-commanding officer at Fort Bragg.

"Sure, Mickke D. I had a funny feeling you were going to call me. What's on your mind?"

I pause and then answer. "Pablo Valdez made another attempt on my life."

"Yeah, I heard. Figured you would get in touch with me. How can I help? But before you answer, you know our government can't get mixed up in local politics in Colombia, right?"

I pause again. "We need to get together and discuss this matter face to face, not over the phone."

"Sure thing, let me see, I'm going to be in Wilmington next Tuesday for a speech. I'll be finished by 1100 hours. Do you want to meet me for lunch?"

I think for a minute and then say, "Great, how about the Lazy Pirate Sports Bar & Grill on Carolina Beach, about noon? I'll e-mail you the address."

The first time I was ever at The Lazy Pirate was when I was still married to my third wife. She took me to a fundraiser there and Danny, the chef and head social director, raised a lot of money that night. We had great burgers for dinner covered in a delicious watermelon relish. I haven't been there in a while so I thought I would give Danny some business.

The colonel replies, "I'll see you there at 1200 hours and you're buying."

"Right, my treat." Why does everyone expect me to buy?

I arrive at the Lazy Pirate about 11:45, say hello to Danny, and of course, Colonel Townsend walks in the door at exactly 12:00. He is a stunning-looking soldier. About 6' tall, 175 pounds, dressed in starched fatigues, spit-shined boots and carrying his beret, he strikes a picture of someone you just know you do not want to tangle with. He is the type of person you just have to stare at, but the minute his eyes meet yours, you blink and look away. He is 10 years older than I am, but he looks 10 years younger than me. We shake hands and his handshake is like putting your hand into a steel vice. It is a lot more fun to salute him than shake his hand.

"So Mickke D, what kind of trouble are you going to get yourself and maybe me into this time?"

"Well Colonel, like I said on the phone, I'm tired of playing defense with Pablo Valdez. He tried to kill me several times in Colombia and now he has made two attempts right here in the States. I've decided it's time for me to go on the offense."

Just as Colonel Townsend starts to open his mouth, our waitress comes over and asks us if we are ready to order. I can't believe my eyes so I stare at her nametag, which is located on a very nice boob, and I am right, I know this girl. "Paula Ann?" I stammer.

"Yes, that's my name and that's my boob you're staring at, now can I take your order?"

"Paula Ann, its Mickke D from Myrtle Beach."

She has a surprised look on her face. "Oh yeah, Mickke D. You're that older guy I went out with a couple of times. 'Pops.' Sure, you used to wear those funny-looking bright red silk boxer shorts. I told all of my girlfriends about them. Yeah, I remember you."

I notice the edges of the Colonel's mouth are starting to curl up. He is getting a huge kick out of this.

"Yeah, right. Thanks for spreading the word around town. So what are you doing working here in Wilmington? I thought you worked at a resort in Myrtle Beach?"

She lets a frown adorn her freckled face. "Oh, I followed my boyfriend up here and then he up and left me and moved to California. I figure I'll stay here for a while and see what happens. I'm taking some college courses and I want to get a degree in psychology."

I am at a loss for words. I have never seen this side of Paula Ann. "Well, nice to see you again and good luck with your studies. Colonel, are you ready to order?"

We give our orders to Paula Ann and as soon as she leaves, Colonel Townsend says, "Mickke D, you've always had a problem with women. I guess some things never change. Isn't she a little young for you and should I refer to you as Pops from now on?"

I can feel my face become flushed as I answer. "Very funny. Hey, she's not that young, and no, don't refer to me as Pops."

Paula Ann returns with our food and as we eat, I tell Colonel Townsend my plan. He listens for a while and then interrupts. "Whoa, Mickke D. If I'm not mistaken, you ended up with a pretty good chunk of change not too long ago. Are you willing to risk all of that just to get back at some drug dealer in Colombia?"

I seize the moment to plead my case. "Well, Colonel, that money won't do me any good if I'm dead, or if I'm constantly looking over my shoulder, waiting for the next attempt on my life. And what about my friends? What if some of them are caught up in an attempt on my life? What if some of them die? How am I going to feel? And besides that, you know me, before making any decision, I look at the best that can happen and the worst that can happen. If I'm not prepared to accept the worst, then I won't do it."

"Okay, I can see I'm not going to change your mind. What do you need from me?"

"I need transportation, weapons, ammo, a rebel fatigue uniform, some local intel, and about three hours on the ground in Colombia."

Colonel Townsend raises his eyebrows. "Is that all? You're planning to do this on your own?"

"Yes I am, it's my fight and no one else's. That's all I can think of right now, but I suspect I'll come up with a few more things before it's time to go."

"Okay, let me see what I can come up with and I'll get back to you. Thanks for lunch, Pops," he says while laughing, and then turns and marches out of the restaurant.

I leave Paula Ann a big tip and one of my business cards. Why I left the card, I do not know. Maybe once she gets her degree, she can help me with some of the demons in my mind.

Chapter 49: Change In Plans

It's Wednesday morning. I asked Jim and Mark to meet me in my office at 10 before I left the office last night. They both walk into the office at about the same time. I motion for one of them to close the door.

"What's up, boss?" Mark asks.

"Guys, whatever is said in this room today stays in this room. Is that perfectly clear?" I say in a very stern voice.

They both nod their heads. I can tell they are surprised by such a blatant serious tone of voice from me. I don't beat around the bush. "I'm going away a week from Friday for a long weekend and I may not return."

"And what does that mean?" Jim asks.

"It means I need to take care of some unfinished personal business out of the country, in a very dangerous part of the world. If for any reason I don't come back, there's a sealed envelope in my desk drawer for each of you. Please follow the instructions in the envelope."

Mark leans back in his chair, crosses his arms over his chest and says, "You're going after Valdez, aren't you?"

"The less you know, the better off you will be," I remark.

Mark hesitates. "Mickke D, you're good, but you can't get to Valdez by yourself. I'm going with you."

"And if he's going, I'm going," Jim says, leaning forward in his chair. "I don't know Valdez but I do know I don't like him."

I'm stunned. I don't know what to say. "And why do you think I would let you two come along?"

"Actually, you don't have a choice, we're in. What's the plan?" Mark whispers, also leaning forward in his chair.

"Mark you have a wife. Jim and I just have ex-wives."

"No Mickke D, you have *ex-wives,* I only have an ex-wife," Jim says and we all laugh.

The laughter seems to break the tension in the room. "Okay, let me make a phone call and we'll meet again for lunch at 11:30."

"You buying?" Jim asks.

"Yeah, I'm buying, we'll go up to Snookey's for lunch."

After Mark and Jim leave my office, I get on my phone and call Colonel Townsend. "Colonel, its Mickke D. I have a question for you."

After a slight pause, he says, "Why do I think I am not going to like your question?"

Ignoring his comment, I ask, "I have two more guys who are going along. You remember Mark Yale? He was with me in Colombia and my neighbor Jim Bolin, a retired FBI agent. I'll need to outfit three instead of just me. Can you handle that?"

"No problem. Sounds like your odds just got a whole lot better. Do they know what you're getting them into?"

"Well, Mark knows, he's been there. Not sure about Jim, but he's a tough guy and he has experience."

"Okay, Mickke D, I will do a set-up for three. E-mail me pants, shirt, and boot sizes. There will be a C-130 landing at the Myrtle Beach International Airport a week from this Friday morning at 0600. It will taxi over to one of the out-of-the-way hangers, Charlie 3. It will take off at 0630. I'll be on board and give everyone the latest intel. Be at Charlie 3 by 0545 and ready to go. I'll see you then."

I take Mark and Jim to lunch at Snookey's in Little River. Snookey's is a neat little restaurant, which is located in a marina along the waterway. You can eat inside or out, depending on the weather. It has a lovely view and the food is excellent.

I pass on the information Colonel Townsend gave me and ask them if they're sure about doing this. They both agree. I tell them our cover here at the beach is that we are going away for a golf weekend and we'll be back in the office on Monday morning.

We are to arrive at the Myrtle Beach Airport dressed like golfers and carrying our clubs. We will leave the clubs in the hanger and pick them up when we return. I pause and add the phrase, "if we return." Neither Mark nor Jim blinks. I guess they are ready.

Chapter 50: The Trip

Friday morning. I say goodbye to Blue and tell him Beverly will be over to feed him and take him for a walk. I pick up Jim and proceed to the office where we pick up Mark around 5 a.m. If anyone sees us, we look just like thousands of other golfers who come to Myrtle Beach each year. The only difference is that instead of coming to the beach to play golf, we are leaving the beach to play golf. One other big difference, each of us has brought along a loaded weapon. Jim checked with his contacts at the airport and found out the best way to get to hanger C-3. We find a place to leave our vehicle, stash our clubs, and wait in silence for the C-130 to arrive.

The cargo plane arrives right on time and taxis up to hanger C-3. The rear cargo door opens and out steps Colonel Townsend, dressed in what looks like the same uniform he had on when I met him at the Lazy Pirate. He shakes my hand, walks over to Mark and says, "Yale, long time, no see. You look good, nice to see you again."

"Thanks Colonel, nice to see you too."

I walk Colonel Townsend over and introduce him to Jim. "Colonel, this is my neighbor Jim Bolin, retired FBI."

"Nice to meet you Bolin. Must be tough living next to this guy."

"You're right, Colonel; there is nothing dull about living next to him."

Out of the corner of my eye, I notice someone exiting from the rear of the C-130. He is dressed in shorts, a T-shirt and flip-flops. I don't recognize the clothes but I could never forget that silver gray hair. It is Bill Cutter, one of my old Army buddies from Fort Bragg.

I am surprised and bewildered beyond belief. I never thought I would ever see this man again. All reports were that he had just disappeared from the face of the earth.

I first met Bill at Fort Bragg when we were part of a weekend golf foursome along with two other Special Forces officers, Barry Green and Ted DeShort. Ted died in a plane explosion and Barry was killed, supposedly, by me. However, there again, that's another story. Let's just say I owe Bill big time.

I walk briskly over to Bill, give him a big hug and shake his hand. "Wasn't sure I would ever see you again. Where have you been hiding?" I ask.

"Ended up in The Bahamas with a lady police detective I met in Charleston. Turned into a beach bum. We have a fishing camp and bed and breakfast down there."

I am still puzzled. "Well, what are you doing here?"

"I've kept in touch with Colonel Townsend and he told me what you were planning. Fishing and being nice to jerks has become rather boring and I needed to get away from the ocean and the little woman for a while. Thought I might tag along with you on one last mission."

Before I have time to answer, Colonel Townsend summons us to meet him inside the hanger. He hands each of us a folder and then says, "First of all, gentlemen, the United States government and the Army has nothing to do with your trip to Colombia. We were never here and you never met us here. If anything happens to you on this trip, we will disavow any knowledge of anything that had to do with this trip. In other words, you are on your own. We are flying from here to The Naval Air Station at Key West. From there we go to Panama City, Panama, where you will pick up a Learjet, which will take you to Valdez's private landing strip in Colombia. The jet is owned by Valdez and he had it flown to Panama to be serviced. He did not trust anyone in Colombia to do it for him. Your pilot will be a retired CIA operative. You will be on the ground for no more than two hours, at which time the pilot will leave with or without you."

He surveys each of us as if waiting for a question before continuing. "Men, inside this folder you will find a blueprint of Valdez's home and a map of the grounds surrounding the home. We have verified there will be seven bodyguards on the property or in the house along with Valdez, his wife, a live-in maid, and two children, a girl, 10, and a boy, 12. You will land on the property at 0200 and as I said before, the plane will leave at 0400 with or without you. We should have satellite coverage for that time period to help with surveillance. I will be with you all the way to Panama and will answer any questions you may have. There are uniforms, weapons, communication devices, food, and drinks onboard. If there are no questions, let's saddle-up and head south."

Chapter 51: The Attack Plan

I have put together a plan of action based on a search-and-destroy mission with three people. Since Bill is also on board, I need to change that plan. I notice he brought his sniper rifle with him so I know exactly what his job will be.

There is a small amount of chatter and banter as the plane is topped off with fuel. As we leave Myrtle Beach International, the reality sets in. All of a sudden, everyone's demeanor changes. Silence takes over the airplane. The only sounds we hear are the hum of the engines. Bill, Mark, and I know the drill and Jim just sort of melds right in with us. We are now at war and we have an enemy to find and destroy.

Colonel Townsend has brought AR-15s with sound-suppressers and night scopes, which were confiscated from Valdez's own people. They are untraceable if left behind. There are also flash grenades, a grenade launcher, which I plan to use on the helicopter supposedly sitting within the compound, and plenty of ammo and magazines. He also has night-vision goggles for all of us. We will all wear gloves so as not to leave any fingerprints. Each of us will wear a black ski mask and a camouflaged floppy hat. We will have no identification of any type on us. There is radio communications equipment, also confiscated in Colombia, so we will have person-to-person contact. Now for the plan.

Colonel Townsend puts up a white board against the fuselage of the plane and with a laser pointer starts his presentation. "Here is what we know as of yesterday. You will be flying into Valdez's private landing strip." He points to a square drawing on his board. "Here is the barracks building where all of the guards are fed and lodged and the extra 4X4s are kept. When you arrive, there should be two guards only at that time. They know the plane is supposed to be returning, but not exactly when, so hopefully it won't cause any panic on their part. There will be two guards stationed at a check point off the main highway on the road into the villa, two guards patrolling the perimeter of the property on 4x4s and one guard at the gate to the compound. The second shift of guards will not arrive until 0500. There should be no one inside the compound with a weapon except Valdez."

Now it's my turn. "Guys, here is my plan. Let me finish and then if you have any comments or ideas, let me know. I will be the first one off the plane and I will eliminate the two guards at the barracks before they have time to alert the other guards and the villa. Bill, I would like you to take one of the 4X4s, skirt the villa and take out the two guards at the road checkpoint. Mark and Jim, I need you to take two 4X4s and find the guards patrolling the perimeter and eliminate them. I will go after the guard at the villa gate and wait for Bill to come and back me up before I go inside. Before leaving the compound, I will take out the helicopter. We will all meet back at the barracks no later than 0400 and go home. If there are any problems, contact me. If I don't answer, call Colonel T."

Mark speaks up. "Do we have any idea how long it takes the guards patrolling the perimeter to make their rounds?"

Colonel Townsend answers, "If they are on schedule, they will leave the barracks at 0130 and it takes them anywhere from 1 hour to 1 ½ hours to make their trip." He points to a red line on his board, which is the trail they normally take.

I break in and point to the board. "If I were you, I would back track and catch them here, pointing to a creek crossing, coming back into the barracks instead of chasing them." Mark and Jim agree.

Colonel Townsend ends the talk, "It's a three-hour trip from Myrtle Beach to Key West, so let's get some rest and we'll discuss the plan again on the flight to Panama."

❧

We are only in Key West long enough to refuel the plane. Our flight time to Panama is about five hours. We arrive in Panama City, Panama around 3, which is 4 their time. We now have time to stretch our legs and bodies. We have access to an empty hanger, which will be Colonel Townsend's command post. There are several computers there along with other sophisticated electronic devices.

We meet our Learjet pilot Rick, who looks more like Jimmy Buffet on his way to a concert than a pilot and ex-CIA operative. We are told that he will also give us some intel since he has actually been on the property. I ask Rick and Colonel T if we shouldn't have a co-pilot. They just stare at me and continue with their conversation.

We are taken to a private firing range where we test fire our weapons and we go over our mission plan one more time before changing into our rebel uniforms, boarding the Learjet and proceeding to our final destination. I say goodbye to Colonel Townsend and thank him for his help.

Rick has a shoulder holster with what looks like a .45 and an AR-15 sitting in the co-pilot's seat. Maybe that's why there is no co-pilot; no room. Rick tells us everything he knows about the villa because he was actually there one time doing an undercover job for the CIA. His recollection pretty much mirrors what Colonel T told us. He did say that Valdez has several weapons in his office and a sawed-off shotgun attached to a swivel under his desk. If I'm lucky, I'll catch him before he has a chance to get to his office.

As soon as we take off, things get very quiet. Bill, Mark and I have been here before. It's the calm before the storm. It's that time in everyone's life when they reflect on their lives and wonder what they might have done differently. It's a time to get mentally ready for the mission. If you're not mentally ready, someone may die and that someone could be you or one of your comrades.

I look at Jim and he gives me a thumbs up. He is ready to go. Mark and Bill have their eyes closed, probably going over their part of the mission in their minds. I close my eyes and go over in my mind what I have to do. The next thing I hear is Rick on the radio telling us ten minutes to touchdown. The demons in my head and stomach are beginning to get restless. It is as if I am returning to a place that I so wanted to rid myself of and hoped I would never see again.

Chapter 52: Boots on the Ground

Pulling the trigger is never easy. Anyone who tells you differently is either a fool or a cold-blooded killer. The act comes with baggage which different people handle in different ways. Sometimes it resonates as fear and sometimes as demons, which may rear their ugly heads at anytime. I have never had a problem with pulling the trigger. Fifteen years ago it was a way of staying alive and just recently it was the same situation, kill or be killed.

We touch down at exactly 1:50 a.m. As we taxi up to the cinderblock nondescript barracks, the barracks door opens and two half-asleep guards walk slowly toward the plane with rifles slung over their shoulders. I watch them approach through a window in the airplane. I do not know them. They are probably married with kids and Valdez gave them a job which probably pays well. At this point in time, those facts do not concern me, or at least I can't allow those thoughts to concern me. If they are not disposed of, they will communicate with the villa, all hell will break loose, and maybe one of my team or I will die.

Rick opens the door to the plane. I fire two shots and the guards fall. Jim and I grab both bodies and drag them into the barracks while Mark, Bill, and Rick cover us. We gather up all the weapons we can find in the barracks and place them on the plane with Rick. The two guards are still breathing so we tape their mouths, tie their hands and feet, and lock them in the bathroom.

The first part of our mission is a success. Rick goes back on board the plane and shuts down the engines so that the engine noise doesn't alarm anyone. He returns and tells everyone to call him when they are heading his way. If he doesn't hear from us, he will initiate power to the plane's engines at 3:45 and leave at 4. If he comes under attack, he will leave immediately and we will be on our own. Not exactly the news you want to hear as you leave on a mission.

Suddenly the radio in the barracks crackles and someone says something in Spanish to the effect of, "Did the boss's plane just come in?"

We all look at each other with confused looks on our faces. Rick grabs the microphone and in what sounds like perfect Spanish answers, "Yes, the plane arrived and there is no problem." He turns the radio off.

We all look at each other and take a deep breath. That radio transmission could be a problem and we just got started. Mark, Jim, Bill, and I go to where the 4x4s are stored and grab one. Colonel T has supplied us with generic noise suppressers for the mufflers on the 4x4s. We attach them. I give everyone thumbs up and we leave. The suppressers work well. Only a mellow whine is audible from the vehicles.

Colonel T told us he did not think the guards had night-vision capability. They will be using lights on the 4x4s, flashlights, and light bulbs for security. We have the advantage. I hope that we will see their lights before they see or hear us.

Jim and Mark take off to intercept the perimeter guards while Bill and I move off toward the villa. We all check our watches. It's 2:14. It's about one mile to the villa on a path about wide enough for one car or truck. We start slowly so our eyes can adjust to the night-vision goggles. In about fifteen minutes, we see a soft glow, which must be lights from the wall surrounding the house and grounds. We slow down and before long the eight-foot high wall is visible. Since light hurts the efficiency of the night-vision goggles, we pull them off and scan the area with our naked eyes. We are on the edge of a wooded area about fifty yards from the wall. The road widens here making travel much easier.

We listen intently for any strange sounds but the night is tranquil and at rest. I whisper to Bill that I will go ahead. He will follow and then after I take out the guard, he will proceed down the road, flank the guard gate off the main road and dispose of the two guards. I remind him to turn off the guard's radios before coming back to the villa. I will wait for him at the gate to the compound. If all goes as planned, he intends to return within about twenty minutes.

❧ ❧

Mark and Jim have reached the creek bed where they set up to ambush the two guards on patrol. They remove their night vision goggles to acclimate their eyes to the surrounding darkness. Mark points to a location where the guards will have to enter on the other side of the creek. They need to attack once the guards reach that point because the guards will be slowing down to cross. They plan to ambush them before they come across the creek to eliminate any chance of Mark and Jim becoming victims of friendly fire. They move the 4x4s off the path and hide them in the underbrush. They take up locations on either side of the trail and wait in silence for the guards to appear. Mark makes sure Jim can see him because he will give the signal to fire. He has already told Jim he will signal and say "fire" just in case it is too dark for Jim to see his signal.

❧ ❧

I maneuver my 4x4 slowly toward the wall looking for any signs of cameras. Colonel T and Rick told us there were cameras on the wall facing the main road into the villa but not on any other part of the surrounding wall. Looks like they were right. Bill will cover me from the wooded area until I give him the signal to come forward. I want to stay as close to the wall as possible. I will use it as a shield until I reach the corner. I will venture the rest of the way on foot.

When I reach the corner of the wall, which turns toward the main gate of the villa and the guard post building, I signal Bill to come up. I watch as he appears out of the wooded area and follows the same path I just followed. Once he is next to me, I dismount from my 4x4, turn the corner on foot, and hug the wall leading to the main gate so the cameras will not detect me. I leave the grenade launcher with Bill. He knows that if something bad happens and I don't make it, he is to blow up the helicopter and return to the guard barracks. I look at my watch. It is 2:40.

> ❧

Mark checks his watch. It is 2:45. They have one hour and fifteen minutes left before the plane leaves with or without them. He hears a faint noise and as he peers down the trail, he can see just the slightest movement of lights. The guards are coming. He clicks his radio one time and Jim returns his click with two clicks. Jim sees them also. The guards are probably a quarter of a mile away. Mark and Jim lock and load, and put their AR-15s on automatic. Both of them can now see the lights of the 4x4s clearly. Their adrenalin begins to spike. Their eyes and ears open wider as their sense of sight and hearing intensify.

> ❧

I make my way to the guard post building positioned at the gate to the compound. I stay as close to the wall as I can. I don't want to be seen by the cameras. When I get to within thirty feet of the gate, I hear a noise and I crouch down. It must have been the sound of a door opening because I hear music. I also hear footsteps and then again I hear what I hope is the sound of a door closing. The music disappears. I stand up and inch forward until I reach the gate. I peer around the corner and see the guard seated at a desk listening to a boom box and gazing at a magazine.

Rick gave me a detailed description of the guard post building. He was very accurate. It is about a 10-foot by 15-foot brick structure with one door. A bank of windows begins about four feet up from the base of the building. There are several computer screens on the desk, which show the guard what the cameras are seeing. There is a small refrigerator and microwave on a table against the far wall.

Rick told me that the gate opens in toward the villa and there is an outside, concealed button which will open the gate in case of an electrical failure. He thinks it's on the inside part of the wall toward the villa. Staying below the windows, I slowly reach through the edge of the gate and find a recessed button. Just as I am about to push it, I freeze. The music has stopped. I can hear footsteps inside the building. I don't have the time to sit here and wait for something to happen. I push the button and the wrought iron gate begins to swing open.

෮෧

Mark and Jim watch as the lights of the perimeter guards 4x4s become larger and brighter. They have almost reached the ambush point on the other side of the creek bed, which is less than twenty yards away. Mark raises his arm and looks at Jim. Jim raises his arm, which tells Mark he is ready. When the guards arrive at the point and begin to slow down, Mark drops his arm and yells, "fire." Mark and Jim unload a full magazine on automatic and the guards never realize what hit them. They fall from the 4x4s as the engines sputter and stop running. The headlights are shattered on their vehicles. The area becomes dark and very quiet.

Mark and Jim position their night vision goggles back on their heads, load another magazine into their weapons, and move slowly toward the creek bed. When they arrive, the guards are not moving. They take their weapons and throw them into the jungle, along with their radios, which they turn off before tossing. They return to their 4x4s, call Rick and tell him they are on their way back to the plane. The time is 3:15. They are on schedule.

෮෧

I stand up and follow the gate as it opens. The guard is completely surprised. As he reaches to set off an alarm which will warn the villa there is an intruder, I fire twice and he drops with his finger on the button. I rush in to the building and move his finger away from the button. Next, I click my radio one time and say, "Go." I watch on the cameras as Bill makes his way down the road toward the last two guards. I check my watch. It's 2:50. Bill should be back no later than 3:15.

෨෧

Mark and Jim arrive back at the barracks and board the plane at 3:35. Now the hard part begins, waiting for Mickke D and Bill to return. Rick is getting antsy. He keeps looking at his watch and fiddling with the switches on the control panel of the plane. He knows that once he fires the engines, the noise could wake everyone in the villa and that is making him terribly nervous.

෨෧

Bill spots the guard shack and after checking his watch, decides he doesn't have time to go around the guards and come up the road and make a frontal attack. He gets off his 4x4 and uses it as a mount for his sniper rifle. He is about fifty yards away from the guard post. He dials in his night scope and yells, "Hey, anyone in there?" Both guards exit the small building with rifles at the ready. They can't figure out what is going on. Bill fires twice. Both guards fall. He climbs back on his vehicle and hurries down to the post. He tosses their weapons and turns off their radios before tossing them. He darts inside and shuts off the main radio to the main gate building and the villa. He scrambles onto his 4x4, clicks his radio, and says, "Be there in five." He checks his watch. It's 3:10.

෨෧

I have been looking around the building while waiting for Bill and I find a file with almost fifty names in it, probably people who are to have access to the villa and Valdez. I figure they are drug lords and distributors. Someone might enjoy having that information. I place the file in my shirt. Just as I receive Bill's message that he is on his way, I notice a light come on and movement from a camera pointed at the villa. This is not good. I was hoping to surprise Valdez.

I leave the building, retrieve my 4x4 and as I am returning, I see Bill coming down the road. We both arrive at the gate about the same time. I tell him about the movement and light. I go back inside the building and turn off every switch I can find. The darkness of night returns as every light in the building and along the wall goes off. We place our night goggles on our heads. It's time for the final assault. I glance at my watch. It's 3:20.

ॐ◦ॐ

Colonel Townsend is nervously pacing back and forth in the hanger back in Panama. He really wanted to go with them, but he knew that was not a possibility. Sometimes it's more difficult to wait than it is to be there. When you're there, time moves much faster. He looks at his watch and it reads 0330. He finally calls Rick, "Have the birds returned to the nest?"

Rick responds, "Two are on their way and no contact with the others."

ॐ◦ॐ

Bill and I move cautiously toward the villa and the one light we can see. As we get closer, more lights come on and our vision is impaired. We stop and remove the night goggles. We dismount from our vehicles and continue on foot. Bill tries looking through the night scope on his rife but to no avail. Suddenly the night is filled with gunfire. Someone is firing at us from the villa. We hit the ground. Bill looks at me and says, "This was sort of fun up till now."

I reply, "Yeah, I guess he knows we're here but I also know he can't see us."

Bill releases the night scope from his rifle and replaces it with another. He says, "Since we don't have a whole lot of time, why don't you draw his fire and maybe I can locate him from the muzzle flash. Besides that, he's probably not a very good shot and he is a long way away."

I look his way and say, "No problem, just don't miss."

I move about twenty yards to my right and call out, "Valdez, its Mickke D, your friend from the USA. This is no way to greet a guest."

Again, several shots are fired in my direction. Then I hear another muzzled shot, which comes from my left. I ask, "So did you get him?"

"Well, I'm pretty sure I hit him, but I don't know where."

I stand up. "I'm going in, cover me, we don't have much time."

This is no time to be cautious. I take off at a trot toward the villa. I think to myself, *I hope there are no dogs and no roots to fall over.* I reach the porch and Bill was right. Valdez is down, shot in the chest but still breathing. He gives me a wry smile. I cock my .45 and point it at his head but for some reason I look up and there are two kids, a boy and a girl, staring at me from a large window. I pause and then look back down at Valdez and say, "If you live, do not send anyone after me again, do you understand? If I have to come back, I will burn this villa to the ground, along with everyone in it, do you understand?"

He barely moves his head in recognition. I turn and jog back to where Bill is waiting. I yell at him, "Blow the copter and let's get the hell out of here, we're almost out of time."

I hear the sound of the grenade launcher and watch as the helicopter goes up in a ball of fire, lighting up the entire area. I gaze back at the villa. I can make out four figures standing over Valdez.

I jump on my 4x4 and we take off at full speed for the plane. I check my watch and its 3:50. I hope Rick is not a prompt person or we're going to have to hunker down and wait for the next bus.

&⊷⊰

At 3:45 a.m., Rick starts the engines to the Learjet. Jim wants to go and find Mickke D and Bill, but Mark tells him to calm down. They still have fifteen minutes. They heard gunfire coming from the area where the villa is located and since the good guys all have silencers, that means the bad guys were not surprised. Five minutes later they hear an explosion and see a large fireball erupt, visible above the tops of the trees.

Now Rick is really getting nervous. He readies the plane for takeoff. Mark says to him, "Don't be in too big a hurry. They still have time to get here."

Rick replies, "They had better hurry, this plane is leaving in five minutes."

Mark pulls his weapon and holds it down at his side. He looks directly at Rick. "This plane is not leaving until they get back here. You saw the explosion. The helicopter was the last thing to be blown. That means they are on their way. Don't be in a rush. We are not leaving without them."

Rick's radio cracks. "Rick, don't leave. We're about five minutes away."

Rick gazes at Mark and the gun in his hand. "Roger that, we'll be here."

Mark holsters his weapon. "See, I told you they were on their way."

Mark and Jim exit the plane and stand guard in case some unexpected guests show up. Within minutes, they see Bill and Mickke D coming toward the plane. Everyone boards and Rick hits the "go" button.

As they take off, they see military vehicles with flashing lights heading up the road toward the compound. Rick banks the plane in the opposite direction and heads for Panama. The time is 4:07.

Once in the air, Bill looks at me and says, "Was he dead?"

I answer immediately but my voice lacks enthusiasm. "Yeah, he was dead, nice shot." I am unable to tell him I couldn't pull the trigger and finish the job.

The remainder of the flight was quiet. I tried to sleep but every time I closed my eyes, I saw those two kids standing in that window. Maybe Paula Ann was right, "Pops" is getting too old for this stuff.

෨෧

We land in Panama and taxi directly into the hanger where Colonel T has set up his headquarters. The hanger doors are closed immediately. Colonel T congratulates us and then gives us the bad news. We can't leave for the States because of bad weather over the Keys so we are debriefed in the hanger instead of on the plane heading home. Everyone is uneasy about staying overnight in a foreign country when you have just attacked one of their neighboring country's largest drug cartel kingpins and confiscated his plane. Luckily, there are no problems.

We leave the next morning at first light for Key West. Before I depart, I thank Rick for waiting for us. He smiles, looks at Mark, and tells me it was an easy decision. He also tells me he's heard good things about Myrtle Beach and that he may just visit sometime. I give him my number and tell him to call anytime.

Once in the air, we all breathe a sigh of relief. I breathe another sigh of relief when Colonel T tells me the attack finally made the papers. He tells me the paper said there had been an early morning terrorist attack on the compound and that they have no suspects at this time. Nothing was mentioned about Valdez being killed in the raid. My inability to pull the trigger may come back to haunt me someday.

Chapter 53: Time to Leave

Friday during their lunch break on the salvage ship, Stephanie gathers her crew on the bow of the ship and breaks the news to them. "Ladies, we are leaving tonight. As soon as we get back to the condo, pack up and be ready to leave by 8. Any questions?"

Jenny, Pat, and Karen are stunned by Stephanie's statement. "Isn't this a little sudden?" Pat says.

"Yes it is, but the quicker we depart, the less chance there is of anyone figuring out what we are doing and when we are doing it."

"So we're sticking to the original plan?" Jenny asks.

"Yes, we are. You guys will be leaving with the boat and I'll take the loot in the U-Haul. I'll meet up with you in the Keys on Sunday night."

"Are you sure you don't want one of us to go with you?" Karen asks.

"No way, end of conservation. We'll discuss the details while we're loading up the U-Haul tonight. Whatever you do, act normal the rest of the day today."

"Won't TC be suspicious when we don't show up tomorrow morning for inventory? That's not giving us much of a head start," Jenny worries.

"No problem. I already told TC we are going to Charleston for a getaway weekend and that we'll do double inventory next Saturday morning. He was fine with that. He said he could use a Saturday off as well. He was going to hire someone to take the guards back and forth all weekend. Therefore, he should not go near the warehouse or his boat until Monday morning. We'll be long gone by then."

ॐॐ

At 8 p.m., the girls leave their rented condo to go to the warehouse. The condo is spotless, not a trace of anything showing they were there. Stephanie made the final inspection and gave the girls her seal of approval. Stephanie and Karen take the U-Haul while Jenny and Pat drive the Tahoe. They drive the U-Haul into the warehouse and close the overhead door. It takes them about two hours to load the truck. They take everything except the really large items. They don't want TC to be left with nothing.

Once loaded, Stephanie drives south toward Charleston. She gives her key to TC's boat to the girls and they drive over to the marina and pick up the boat. The guard on duty knows them and once they tell him they're all going for a moonlight cruise, he doesn't question their intentions. The boat is full of fuel. TC tops it off every night when they come back to shore. They also head south toward Charleston, staying within sight of the shore at all times. The girls know their way around boats so they have no problem with TC's. He was always more than willing to let them steer the boat on their trips to and from the salvage ship. Stephanie's plan is to have the authorities follow the boat and not her in the truck.

They know exactly where they are going. Stephanie called ahead and made all of the arrangements. The girls' first stop is a small marina just north of Charleston where they sell TC's boat, "The Judge," for $150,000 in cash to some rather unscrupulous people who within an hour have changed the name from "The Judge" to "Hannah's Fantasy" and by Monday morning, it has an entirely new paint job. They produce a fake bill of sale and by Tuesday, they have sold the boat for $300,000 to an online buyer from Saudi Arabia, who will be flying in on Friday to pick up the boat. Karen, Jenny, and Pat pocket $50,000 in cash each, and then they rent a boat from the same people and proceed to Key West where they are to meet Stephanie, split up the rest of the money from the sale of the artifacts, and then go their separate ways.

The girls arrive in Key West Sunday around noon. They made very few stops along the way, only for fuel, food, and to stretch their sea legs. They were told where to leave their rental boat and they encounter no problems. They proceed to Mallory Square to meet up with Stephanie. They all agreed to refrain from making any calls on their cell phones until they are out of the country. None of the girls have ever been to Key West, so they are pleasantly surprised by the laid-back atmosphere. It's a nice break from their ten-hour days, mostly underwater. They each have a bag full of money to spend and the promise of more to come.

5 p.m. comes and goes and no Stephanie. The girls decide to get a nice hotel suite on Duval Street and wait there. They will take turns waiting for Stephanie at Mallory Square. They have a great dinner and Jenny takes the first two-hour watch at Mallory Square. Karen relieves her at 8 and Pat takes the shift from 10 to midnight.

≈⊰

The girls are going to have a long wait. Stephanie has gone to Plan B. Her original plan has fallen apart and it's all because some spineless British captain back in the early 1700s decided to bury his ship's bounty on land, God only knows where, instead of just shooting the leaders of a proposed mutiny and proceeding on his merry way. She now has no chests full of gold and silver, no jewels from across the seven seas, and no ironclad retirement program. She plans to eventually return to the Grand Strand and find the buried treasure if TC doesn't find it first, but for now she must be content with what she has.

She takes the battery out of her phone and tosses her cell phone as soon as she gets out of Pawleys Island. She drives to Georgetown, gets a motel room and spends the rest of the night there. She sleeps in until 9 and then drives down to Savannah. She meets her contact, shows him the contents, and sells the truck full of artifacts for one million dollars. With gun in hand, she gets on her laptop and waits until the money is transferred to her overseas account before she hands over the keys of the U-Haul. Next, she goes to the airport and with a fake passport and drivers license, she purchases a one-way ticket to Antigua.

She is not concerned about her crew. If they did as she told them to do, they will each have $50,000 cash in their pockets and hopefully enough sense that when she doesn't show up to get the hell out of there and out of the country before they end up on a no-fly list.

ॐॐ

Pat returns around midnight and the girls have a meeting. Pat starts the conversation. "I think we've been stood up. Have any of you ever known Stephanie to be late for anything?"

Jenny answers. "Never, I think you're right, we've been had."

"So now what do we do?" Karen asks.

Pat seems to take over as the person in charge. "I think we should call the airport right now and find out when the first flight is out of the country. We need to get the hell out of here. TC will find out what happened tomorrow morning and they will start searching for us. It won't take long for them to put us on a no-fly list. Does everyone have their fake passport and driver's license?"

Karen and Jenny shake their heads affirmatively. Pat makes the call to the airport. The first flight out of the country leaves tomorrow morning at 6:00 for Cancun. There is another one at 6:20 leaving for Barbados and one leaves at 6:45 for the Caymans. Karen books the Cancun flight, Pat the flight to the Caymans and Jenny books the Barbados flight. None of the girls get much sleep the rest of the night. They catch a taxi to the airport and all leave without a hitch. Before they leave, they make a pact. The first one to see Stephanie will kill her. They all agree.

Chapter 54: Liz and Stan

Liz Woodkark's private/secure phone rings. Liz is the head of a splinter, covert faction of the CIA. She is funded by seized drug money and confiscated material items such as boats, houses, and cars. The intelligence business runs on covert money. She has several blind accounts that she uses for outside payments, contract help, and that sort of thing. She answers only to the director of the CIA and that is not very often.

The caller is Stan Hutchinson, her ex-Seal undercover CIA operative and golf junkie.

"Stan, I guess you got my message. I hope I didn't take you away from your golf game."

Stan hesitates and then replies, "Yes, I got your call and no I'm not playing golf. What can I help you with?"

"Any news from Beverly about that Mickke D guy? Does she think he could work out as an operative, maybe even on an as needed, part-time basis?"

"Come on Liz, she's sleeping with the guy. Do you think she's going to take a chance and blow her cover by asking that question? Besides that, the guy is rich. According to her, he doesn't need the money."

"So what has she told you?"

"Well, you already know about him attempting to track down a serial killer in the Myrtle Beach area, and that he also killed two guys who tried to kill him on his way to his back doctor's appointment, and that he and a friend have been doing some treasure hunting for the state off the coast of Pawleys Island. Latest is that he is still doing PI work in the Myrtle Beach area. She did tell me he was away for three days with two other guys from his office, supposedly playing golf, but she wasn't sure where. When they got back to the office, they looked tired, they were unshaven and there was not a lot of conversation about the trip, which is sort of strange for guys who go off on a golf weekend."

Liz is searching for information but seems to be getting nowhere. "So Stanley, what about the Valdez cartel in Colombia? Have you been able to get anyone on the inside yet?"

Stan knows that when Liz calls him Stanley, she is upset with him. "Not yet. They're a close-knit family, but I'm working on it. Voice traffic has become very quiet down there all of a sudden. There was some sort of a raid on the compound and the news is sketchy to say the least."

"Well Stanley, I have a news flash for you, Senior Valdez and seven of his guards were killed two nights ago in that early morning raid. And here's the kicker, everyone was killed except the women and children. Also, no one is claiming the kill."

"Then it wasn't drug related or they would have killed everyone and made it public," Stan says. After no reply from Liz, he sheepishly asks, "You don't think Mickke D had anything to do with that, do you?"

"Don't know Stanley, didn't you tell me that Beverly told you Mickke D had a bounty on his head from some Colombian drug cartel kingpin and that he figured it was that same cartel who sent the guys who tried to kill him on the way to his appointment? Maybe he was playing golf in Colombia." She slams the phone down before Stan has a chance to answer.

Stan Hutchinson had recruited Beverly and one of her jobs was to take over his position as the main recruiter for Liz's Southeastern cells. Liz has covert cells all over the world and each one has its own agenda. Most individuals end up going deep undercover until Liz gives them the word that the time has come.

Beverly has two objectives for being in the Myrtle Beach area. First, she is to try to recruit Mickke D to work as a part-time agent for Liz, and secondly there is someone in the area who Liz needs eliminated. Liz knows the person is in the Myrtle Beach area but she does not know his or her identity.

Beverly doesn't mind doing either job. Getting close to Mickke D has had its benefits, and living in Myrtle Beach has been great. She loves the ocean and the beach. Liz hopes that Beverly hurries along with recruiting Mickke D because once she gets the name of the person to eliminate, and Beverly does the job, she will leave Myrtle Beach for another location. She has told Beverly several times not to get romantically involved while on the job, to remember this is just a job and not a permanent address. Once again, she didn't listen.

Beverly's real name is Samantha Miller and she was born and reared in Wrangell, Alaska. Wrangell is a small island located in the southeastern part of Alaska along the Inland Passage. Population of less than 1,500 inhabitants, Samantha grew up with parents who taught her to live off the land, to hunt, fish, and kill to provide for her in the harshest of situations. She is a survivalist.

Stan Hutchinson met her on a fishing trip to Wrangell. Of course, Wrangell had the only golf course in Southeast Alaska. Stan took his golf clubs as well as his fishing gear. How many people can say they played golf in Alaska while on a fishing trip? When he returned to the lower 48, he contacted Liz and she flew up to meet Beverly. Liz offered her a career, a great salary, and a chance to see the world. She received a new identity, left Alaska, and has never been back. Her parents and family think she died in a plane crash over the Cook Islands. She has been with Liz for almost thirteen years now. One might say she is a CIA agent in the Witness Protection Program.

Chapter 55: The Girls Are Gone

Monday morning, my cell phone rings. It's TC. "Mickke D, we have a big problem."

I love it when people begin a conversation by saying *we* have a problem when what they really mean is *they* have a problem. "TC, you have no idea what a real problem is."

"No seriously, are you sitting down?"

"Yes, TC, I'm sitting down. I had a rough couple of weeks. Now tell me what's wrong."

He begins to ramble. "I went to the marina to get my boat this morning and it was gone, then I went over to the warehouse where everything from the Queen Beth was being stored and just about everything of value was gone. The warehouse was almost empty. Someone stole my boat and everything of value we had salvaged so far from the Queen Beth."

"TC, you're right, you do have a problem. But, hey, don't you have the boat insured?"

"Of course I do, but what do I tell our friends in Columbia, you know, the people who are paying the bills?"

"Let me ask you this. Where is your salvage crew, you know, the girls who know all about your boat and where everything is stored?"

Silence. "I can't find them either. Security at the marina said the girls came by about 11 to take the boat out for a moonlight cruise and they never came back. You don't think they had any-thing to do with this, do you?"

"Well unless someone stole your boat, took what you had found, and kidnapped your crew, I'd say it's a real good possibility."

"So now what do we do?"

I hesitate and then answer. "Let me get some things taken care of here and then I'll be down. Call the police and report your boat stolen, but don't say anything about the storage area. And by the way, don't tell me the girls had access to your boat keys and the key to the warehouse."

"Well, sort of. I'll see you when you get here. Meet me at the marina."

"So they could have a one-day jump on us if they took everything Saturday night, does that sound right?"

"Well, they could have taken everything Friday night because Stephanie called and said they would not be available on Saturday for inventory. She was going to take the crew to Charleston for a weekend getaway, so I took the weekend off also, and went out and played golf. I never went to the marina or warehouse the entire weekend."

I just shake my head as I hang up the phone.

સ્જી

At the marina, TC shows me a note that Stephanie left for him at the marina front desk in a sealed envelope which says, "Sorry TC. I'll take this part of the salvage and since I didn't have time to find the buried treasure on land, maybe you will. Do your bosses in Columbia know about the treasure map you found at the site of the Queen Beth? And by the way, nice boat."

I stare at him and say, "How did they know about the map?"

"I never told anyone but you about the map. They had to have been in my house and opened my safe."

"Well, has your house been broken into lately?"

"Well, maybe, maybe not. I'm not sure but I think someone may have been in my house several weeks ago. But the safe was locked and nothing was missing."

"So, did you call the police this morning after talking to me?"

"Yes I did and I told them how they can locate my boat."

I get a funny look on my face. "And how will they do that?"

"When I thought someone had been in my house, I broke down and had an alarm system put in and the security company also hid a GPS responder on the boat. I gave the police the code, so as long as whoever stole my boat didn't find the bug and disable it, the police should be able to trace the boat wherever it goes.

እ–ৰ্চ

South Carolina Governor Melissa Craig makes her bi-monthly call to Judge Cadium for an update on the progress of the salvage job off the coast of Pawleys Island.

"Judge Cadium, this is Governor Craig. How are things going on the Queen Beth?"

TC has no idea how to answer. "Governor Craig, good to hear from you. We've had some new issues pop up, nothing serious, and as soon as I get these issues resolved I'll get back to you."

"Well, okay, keep me advised."

TC just bought himself maybe two weeks to find the missing artifacts from the Queen Beth.

እ–ৰ্চ

Friday morning just north of Charleston, the Saudi business-man who bought TC's boat online walks into the marina office and introduces himself. He tells the manager he would like to see the boat before final confirmation of the transfer of funds. They walk out the front door and three South Carolina State Patrol officers confront them. They display their badges and one of them steps forward and says, "We are looking for a stolen 46-foot Carver and we think it's in your marina."

The manager turns to run back into the office but another officer blocks the door. The manager raises his hands and the Saudi just shakes his head.

During questioning, the manager tells the agents about the phone call from an unknown woman and about the three women who delivered the boat. Of course, by this time Stephanie and her crew have all left the country.

The state patrol calls TC and tells him they have his boat, which now has a new paint job and a new name.

Chapter 56: Beverly Is Missing

It's Wednesday morning around 10 and I get a call from Jim at the office. "Hey, is Beverly at your place?"

"No, I haven't seen her since yesterday. Why, what's going on?"

Jim sounds concerned. "Well, she didn't show up this morning. I called her cell and no one answered."

"Okay, I'm about ready to leave. I'll stop by her place on the way in."

Before I leave the house, I try calling her cell but it just keeps ringing, never going to voicemail. I drive over to her Tillman Resort condo in North Myrtle Beach and her leased Lexus is in the parking garage. I asked her several times how she could afford that car and the condo she was living in. I knew it wasn't from what I was paying her. She said her home computer business was doing well.

I go up to her corner condo on the sixth floor and ring the bell. No one answers the door. I try opening the door, but it is locked. I call out her name and still no response. I go back downstairs to the front desk and ask the girl on duty for a key to her condo. I explain that I'm concerned she may be sick or injured.

After calling and getting no answer, the young lady finally agrees to go with me and unlock the door. She opens the door and we walk in. Except for the furniture that was already there, the place is empty. All of her personal items are gone and her two cats are nowhere to be seen.

The girl finally says, "I don't believe this. She signed a lease. She can't just up and leave. I have a signed lease."

I look at her with a blank stare and before I can say anything, my phone rings. It's Detective Concile. "Mickke D, I have a news flash for you. One of your serial killer suspects was shot and killed last night in the parking lot at Night Fever in Myrtle Beach."

Still perplexed, I answer, "No kidding. Who was killed?"

"Terry Graff. He was sitting in the front seat of his car with a bullet hole in his head. We talked to the manager of the club and she said she remembered him. He left with a younger woman, maybe mid-to-late thirties, blond pixie hair and a short skirt. She also said the lady had great legs."

I nonchalantly reply, "I guess I won't have to interview Mr. Graff. Thanks, detective."

I just keep gazing around the condo with my phone to my ear. There is nothing left that even barely implies that Beverly was living here. It's as if she never existed.

"Mickke D, are you still there? Are you okay?"

"Yes, detective. I'll get back to you." I close my phone.

On my way downstairs, I call Jim. "Jim, you're not going to believe this. Beverly's gone, her personal things are gone and the cats are gone. The condo is empty except for the basic furniture and from what I can tell, someone sent in a cleaner to make sure the place was spotless and print free."

Jim responds, "Wow, I told you, sounds like CIA or Witness Protection."

Chapter 57: The Hit

Terry Graff keeps noticing this really hot chick at the bar. She will occasionally look his way and smile. He cannot figure out if she is a pro or just likes him. He definitely is not paying for it, no matter how hot she looks.

Not being a shy guy, he goes over to her and with a big smile starts a conversation. After a couple of beers for him and a glass of Chardonnay for her, he invites Kathy to leave the club with him and go to Patio's for a nightcap. She says she has never been there and it sounds like fun.

Once in the car Kathy asks, "Well, Terry, what do you do for a living? You look much too young to be retired."

"I retired early from the IRS and I made some good investments along the way. What do you do?"

With a stern look on her face, she replies, "I kill people."

Terry turns and looks at her. His smile disappears.

She laughs. "Oh, I'm just kidding. I have a home-based computer business. You should have seen the look on your face, works every time."

Terry is beginning to wonder if this is a good idea. Kathy may not have both oars in the water.

"Terry, I heard about some retired people who were bilked out of their life savings by an ex-IRS agent. Some of the victims actually committed suicide and the remainder of them were too ashamed of their stupidity to bring charges against the guy or ever reveal his name."

Terry is no longer smiling. "I don't know anything about that and you know what? I don't think I want to go to Patio's. I think I'm just going to call it a night."

Kathy never blinks. "Well, you know Terry, there comes a time in everyone's life when you just have to pay the piper for your indiscretions and guess what? Today is your day. Oh, and I was not kidding before, I do kill people, but only bad people."

She quickly retrieves her 9mm Glock 29 with a silencer from her over-sized purse and before Terry can say or do anything, she puts it to his head and says, "Liz sends her love." She pulls the trigger.

She removes her pixie wig, takes out a pair of rolled-up slacks from her purse and changes from short skirt to pants. She wipes down any part of the car she might have touched and calls a cab, which is how she got here in the first place. She walks down to the CVS to wait for her cab.

She has the cab drop her off two blocks away from the resort. She walks to her condo, grabs her bags and cats, loads everything into a waiting black Chevy Tahoe with tinted windows. The SUV transports her to the Grand Strand Airport where a private plane is waiting to take her to Atlanta, her new home. As the plane takes off, she peers out the window and a tear flows down her cheek. She does not enjoy leaving Myrtle Beach, Mickke D, her friends at the office, and of course, Blue. This had been her longest stay in one place and Liz had warned her about getting involved. Liz was right. She seriously thought about telling Mickke D the truth about what she does but she did not think he would have understood. It's better to just leave and start over somewhere else. This time she is going to listen to Liz and not get involved. She turns away from the window and closes her eyes. Myrtle Beach is now her past and Atlanta is her future.

Chapter 58: Dead Suspect

I arrive at the office and sit in the parking lot for a few minutes before going inside. I still can't believe Beverly just up and disappeared from the face of the earth. She was actually beginning to grow on me. Maybe not enough to become my fourth wife but we had a lot of good times together.

I go inside and see Jannie, Mark's wife, at the front desk. Jim must have called her to come in and work the reception desk.

"Did you find Beverly?" She asks.

"No, not yet Jannie."

I go directly to Jim's office. He peers over the top of his glasses. "How are you doing? Are you okay?"

"Yeah, I'm fine. Can the CIA or Witness Protection actually move someone that quickly?"

"Oh yes, they are excellent at that."

"While I was at her condo, Detective Concile called and said one of my suspects was killed last night at Night Fever and she said it looked like an execution."

He looks up. "Was it your friend Larry Meggart?"

"No, it was Terry Graff."

He motions for me to close the door. "That's interesting because I just got some info back from the Bureau this morning. You know you asked me to check with my contacts at the Bureau to see if they had any info on your suspects. It is not public info but the FBI was looking into him as heading a scam where hundreds of senior citizens were bilked out of their life savings. Several of the seniors committed suicide and the rest refused to name him or sign a complaint because they did not want to admit they had been stupid enough to fall for his scam."

I take a seat. "Would the CIA take him out?"

"No, not directly, but you know what? While I was still with the Bureau, there was a rumor going around the office that the CIA had several special covert cells set up to do just that, but we couldn't find anything factual on the subject and an investigation was never started."

I am becoming more amazed by the second. "So, do you think Beverly could have been part of a covert cell?"

"Well, your suspect, who probably deserved it, gets killed last night and Beverly disappears last night. If I was right about her being CIA, it is very possible. Stranger things than that have happened my friend, much stranger things."

Chapter 59: Gone Fishing

Jon Barry, now living in North Myrtle Beach, is a retired cop from New York City and he is on his way to a new fishing spot. Jon is eighty years old, in good health with a full head of snow-white hair. Jon has a gift for gab; he is always talking about fishing to whoever will listen to him. He plays an occasional round of golf but he would rather fish than play golf anytime.

Jon has a top-of-the line fishing boat, a 19.5' Nitro Z-7 Sport with trailer he purchased at Bass Pro Shop in Myrtle Beach. The boat is equipped with a 250 XL OptiMax Pro XS motor, a trolling motor, and an 1198c SI Combo fishfinder imaging system. He also purchased a new pick-up truck to haul his boat and trailer.

Jon was at the Oyster Bay Golf Course a few days ago to play his monthly round of golf and naturally got into a conversation about good places to go fishing along the Grand Stand with one of the guys who works there. His new fishing buddy friend told him about a hard-to-find, out-of-the way spot out off of Route 9 toward Loris called Billybob Swamp. He told him the bass are huge and as long as you have a boat and a good truck, you'll probably catch your limit in no time.

Its 7:30 in the morning and Jon is weaving his way through the swamp and finally arrives at his new, although not proven, bass paradise fishing hole. He brought with him a thermos of hot coffee and a mid-morning sandwich for a snack. If he gets too busy catching fish to eat his sandwich, he'll feed it to the fish before he leaves.

He unloads his boat and slowly, with the help of his trolling motor, moves out into the swamp. The lake looks to be at least twenty to thirty acres of calm, smooth, brackish water. He notices an occasional cypress tree growing in what looks like shallow water. He also notices several alligators on the far bank basking in the early morning sun but they don't seem to see him. Jon has never fished in a swamp before so he did ask his friend about alligators. His friend told him he has never had a problem with the gators, but just to be safe, be sure and keep all of your extremities inside the boat.

Jon turns on his fishfinder and starts gazing at the screen, looking for the big one. The depth of the water is running anywhere from eight feet to fifteen feet as he ventures out into the lake. It takes a while to get the screen adjusted for the murky water but after about ten minutes, he can make things out pretty well. About ten minutes later, he notices both of the alligators, which were on the bank, are now missing. They must have quietly slipped into the water. Jon always has a weapon on board and he checks his gun to make sure it is loaded. He puts his favorite bass lure on and cast it out into the calm water for the first time.

As soon as his lure hits the water, Jon makes himself comfortable in his fishing seat on the bow of his boat. His medium depth "wobbler" slowly sinks and then Jon reels it in at a slow to medium pace. When the lure gets to within thirty feet of his boat, he feels the tug of a bite. He sets the lure, and what looks like at least a two-pound largemouth bass comes to the surface and does a tail spin across the water. Jon is elated. First cast, big bass. *This is great,* he thinks. *It doesn't get any better than this.* He slowly reels the fish in, relishing in the effort the fish makes to break loose from the alien object in its mouth. He carefully removes the barbed hook and takes a picture of the fish. He then prepares to release the fish back into the water for another fisherman to catch someday.

Just as Jon is releasing the fish, the water next to his boat explodes. One of his alligator friends snatches the bass and almost Jon's hand. He jumps back from the edge of the boat and reaches for his gun. He notices a large head and two wide-set eyes pop up out of the water. The alligator arches his neck upward and swallows the fish. The alligator then disappears into the brackish black water. Within seconds, he is back, almost twenty feet away, watching him. Jon calms down and then begins to laugh. He puts his weapon away and says to the gator, "If you think I'm going to feed you bass all day, you're mistaken."

Jon decides that the next fish will go into the livewell on his boat and he will release the fish when the gator is not around. He continues his fishing and the gator continues to watch. After about thirty minutes and no hits on several of his best lures, he checks his fishfinder and it is showing nothing. He thinks the fish got the word that a hungry gator is on the prowl. He opts to move back closer to shore. As the boat moves forward, powered by his trolling motor, the alligator disappears from view but Jon has a funny feeling he did not go very far.

As he gets closer to shore and just out from where he launched his boat, he cast his lure and it immediately becomes snagged. He tugs on the line and lets the boat drift to where the lure is hung up. When he is right over the spot, he checks his fishfinder to see what has captured his lure. He cannot believe his eyes; it looks like the lure is hung up on a car sitting on the floor of the swamp.

He spent enough time as a cop to figure out that most cars probably do not do well in swamps. He knows there are several possibilities. The car could have just been abandoned by its owner, or it could be a car that was used in a robbery or other felony. He decides to call the police. He makes the 911 call from his cell phone and waits for the authorities to arrive. He cuts the fishing line and attaches a float to the line in the water to mark the spot of the car. He takes his boat out of the water and moves it and his pick-up out of the way so there is a clear path down to the water.

The rescue squad arrives in about thirty minutes, towing a boat. Jon introduces himself and points to the bright orange float marking the spot where the car is located. He also tells them about the alligators, and how one of them almost took his hand off. The divers thank him for the information and retrieve the electric prods from their truck. They get Jon's contact information, tell him he can leave, and thank him for the call. Jon says to them, "If you can get my lure back, I would appreciate you calling me. I've caught a lot of bass with that lure."

The divers look at each other and grin. They tell him they will give him a call if they can save his lure.

Chapter 60: First Big Break

Detective Sam Concile receives a call around 11:30 a.m. It is from the County Rescue Squad. They have pulled a car from Billybob Swamp which may match the car driven by Ellen Thorn, one of her missing persons. Sam yells at Woolever and Statten to saddle up, that there may be a break in the missing persons case.

They arrive at Billybob Swamp thirty minutes later. Sergeant Hoehandle from the County Rescue Squad meets them and gives Sam the latest update. "Looks like the same make and model you put out on the wire. Probably been in the water for three or four weeks."

"Any bodies?" Sam asks.

"Well, yes and no. We didn't find any bodies in the car, but it looks like there may have been bodies at one time. We found a few parts here and there." He points to the two alligators over on the far bank. "I think those two guys over there may have destroyed any evidence of a body. They look pretty plump to me."

"You mean you think they ate the bodies?" Woolever says, eyes wide.

"Wouldn't surprise me a bit. If you want to find out for sure, we can shoot them and check out their stomach contents."

Sam changes the subject. "Sergeant, you said yes and no. What about the yes?"

"Well, we also found two rolled up tarps on the floor of the swamp with cinder blocks tied to them. There were bodies inside. The gators had not gotten to them yet."

"Male or female?"

"Looks like both were female. We'll know more once we get them back to the morgue, but they haven't been in the water as long as the car, maybe a week or two. So do you want us to shoot the alligators?"

Sam pauses. "I don't think we have a choice right now. Do it."

Sergeant Hoehandle gives Sam his business card and Jon Barry's contact information. She thanks him for the call and tells him to keep her advised as to what they find.

It is a quiet trip back to the beach. Sam knows she cannot keep this out of the papers and she is afraid the killer will run. At least if he does run, the killing should stop. However, will it start again somewhere else? She needs to stop this serial killer now. She tells Woolever and Stratton to put eyes on all of the remaining suspects on Mickke D's list, just in case he was right. She wants to know if any of them try to leave town.

Once she gets back to the office, and since lunch does not sound very appetizing right now, she decides to call Mickke D.

ॐॐ

My phone rings. It's Sam. "Mickke D, we've had a break in the missing persons case."

"Fantastic, what happened?"

She fills me in with everything they learned at Billybob Swamp and that the car they found matched the description of Ellen Thorn's vehicle. She also told me about the two bodies they found wrapped up in the tarps and weighted down with cinder blocks. There could be a total of four; Ellen, Jack, Page, and Paula German.

"How did you find out about the swamp?" I ask.

She replies, "Some guy was fishing and got his lure snagged on something. When he looked at his fishfinder to see what had snagged his lure, he spotted the car. He is a retired New York City cop. He called 911."

"Were there any bodies in the car?"

"No, the sergeant with the rescue squad said he thinks alligators may have destroyed the bodies. They are going to shoot the gators and check the contents of their stomachs for evidence."

"Wow, what a lucky break. When is the news going to hit the paper?"

"Not sure. I hope not until we have the autopsy results from the coroner's office and if they find any evidence in the gators."

"So, do you think the killer will run once the news gets out?"

"Don't know, but I am keeping an eye on your three remaining suspects just in case."

"Thanks detective, I still think one of them is involved."

I plan to keep asking questions as long as she continues to answers them. "Are you going to interview Mr. Barry?"

"Probably not, he was just in the right place at the right time and he was an ex-cop, so he made the call."

"Say, do you mind if I go out and have a look around? I promise to stay out of everyone's way."

"Sure, but wear old shoes, it's very wet out there. I'll meet you there in about an hour." She gives me the coordinates for my GPS.

☜☞

I arrive within an hour and find Detective Concile. She introduces me to Sergeant Hoehandle and he fills me in with the details. I have an up-close and personal overall view of Billybob Swamp and the crime scene. I return to Detective Concile and ask, "Would you mind if I talked to Mr. Barry?"

"Of course not, knock yourself out, however......."

Before she can finish her sentence, I say, "I know. If I find out anything, let you know right away."

She shakes her head in a negative manner and gives me Jon Barry's contact information. I figure it will not hurt to speak with him, particularly since he is a retired cop. On the ride back to my office, I am trying to figure out why Sam is being so cooperative. When I first met her, she acted as if I had the plague but now it's as if she wants my help. Does she have an alternative motive?

☜☞

I arrive back at the office, find Jim and give him an update. I then place a call to Mr. Barry. Once he answers, I tell him who I am and that I got his number from Detective Concile, who got it from the rescue squad. Jon tells me he is more than willing to help me if he can.

"Why did you decide to go fishing in Billybob Swamp?" I ask him.

"Well, I was playing golf at Oyster Bay the other day and started talking to one of the guys who works there about fishing. He suggested I try my luck at the swamp."

"What is the name of your friend at Oyster Bay? I may want to talk to him also."

"Oh, let me think, his name was Ed Klink. I remember kidding him about Colonel Klink on that old TV show *Hogan's Heroes*. I'm sorry but I don't have a phone number for him but he told me he works there three or four days a week at the bag drop."

I thank Jon and tell him I'll be back in touch.

Chapter 61: Missing Persons No More

Two days later, Detective Concile gets her anticipated call from the coroner's office. They did find remains in the car of two separate bodies, one male and one female. Both of the bodies that they discovered in the two rolled-up tarps were females and they both had been stabbed in the abdomen, just like Jennifer Holmes, prior to their entombment in the swamp. The rescue squad shot the two gators from the crime scene and brought them to the coroner's office. The coroner opened them up and both of the gators had jewelry and a watch inside their stomachs. He is sending everything over to her by courier ASAP.

The story hits the news channels and the newspapers the day following the find in the swamp. *So far, none of Mickke D's three remaining suspects have tried to leave town. Maybe the killer was Terry Graff and the killings will stop,* she thinks. *However, I don't believe a serial killer would be caught off guard by someone and killed in their own car in a parking lot.*

☙☙

Sam receives the contents from the coroner's office later that afternoon. As soon as she gets the evidence, she calls Cathy Jay and asks her if she could come by the station to see if she can identify any of the jewelry or watches. Cathy arrives within an hour and recognizes a ring that Ellen always wore and she thinks one of the watches looked like Ellen's. Cathy is visibly upset. Sam thanks her for stopping by and giving a positive identification of the jewelry.

Sam is now sure in her own mind that the bodies in the car were Ellen and Jack. Now the only question is who killed them.

The other two women have been tentatively identified as Connie Smith and Page Rivers. Was Jennifer Holmes one of his victims, as well? What kind of a human being could do something like this to another human being? This is one part of police work Sam will never get used to.

Chapter 62: Witness Interview

The day after I speak with Mr. Barry, I grab Jim and we take a ride out to Oyster Bay. I have no problem talking Jim into going with me once I tell him where we are going. I'm not sure what we will find at the golf course, but I do feel we are getting close to the killer.

Once we arrive, I ask Jim to keep his eyes open and to be ready for anything. I go directly over to the bag drop and ask for Ed Klink. Someone points to a tall slender man probably in his late fifties who is unloading bags from an SUV. I wait until he is finished unloading the golf clubs, then I go over to him, hand him my card, and introduce myself.

"Mr. Klink, my name is Mickke MacCandlish and I am a private investigator. Would you mind answering some questions for me? It pertains to the ongoing investigation out at Billybob Swamp."

He quickly answers, "I could not believe that when I read about it in the paper. I fish out there all the time but I never use a fishfinder. I'm old-fashioned and just use my wits. I get a break in about fifteen minutes. I'll meet you in the restaurant, if that's okay."

I tell him that's fine. Jim and I go over to the restaurant and order a cup of coffee. Jim doesn't stay long. He tells me he will be in the pro shop if I need him. I take a table close to the window where I can keep an eye on Mr. Klink. At this point in my investigation, everyone is a suspect. I can feel my demons beginning to raise their ugly heads and looking around for a way out. I drench them with hot coffee.

Chapter 63: The Hunter

The hunter has pretty much lived a charmed life. He has never been confronted by anyone at any time. He grew up with low self-esteem and started being a bully in grade school. He felt powerful when he could hurt others. Since he started this behavior early in school and it went unchecked, he grew into a nasty adult. All throughout his time in his government job, no one ever called his bluff. He always had the ability and the balls to control people in any situation. He was always in charge.

Sex may have been the only exception. He could never understand why they would not do exactly as he wanted them to do. He enjoyed rough and varied sex and he thought that his partner should just give in and do whatever he wished. It didn't take long for most of his female friends to figure out that he was a little strange and very seldom did any of them return for a second date. Before he met his dead ex-wife, he pretty much paid for sex, and there were even a few of those girls who refused to go back for a second go around. His wife had a kinky side to her but even she got tired of his brand of rough sex after a while.

He has transitioned into a psychopathic killer. He just doesn't care, and he has learned to mimic human emotion to pass among the unknowing and to lure his prey. The thing that makes him a top-of-the-line killer and chameleon is his ability to become the man he is pretending to be.

However, now he has a new problem. Some yahoo old fart fishing in Billybob Swamp gets his lure snagged on a car and now the authorities have discovered his underwater cemetery. What are the odds of that ever happening? How long is it going to take them to put two and two together and figure out he is the killer?

There's only one person who can link him to the swamp and that is Ed Klink. He figures he had better eliminate Ed before anyone gets a chance to talk to him. He goes to the golf course and he no sooner gets there when he sees Mickke D with another fellow talking to Ed.

Why is Mickke D talking to him and not the police? Maybe the police have not put the puzzle together. Has Mickke D figured it out? He stays in his pick-up truck and watches as Mickke D and the new guy leave Ed and walk toward the clubhouse. He attaches a silencer to his weapon.

Chapter 64: The Hunter No More

I watch as Mr. Klink walks my way from the bag drop. He gets about halfway to the door when all of a sudden his knees buckle and he falls down. Several people in the area rush over to where he is lying, and then one of them yells out, "This man's been shot!"

This sets off complete chaos. People are looking around and running for cover. For some reason, I notice a pick-up truck slowly pull out of the parking lot and leave the golf course.

I call for Jim and he quickly appears from the pro shop. "What happened?"

"I think our killer just shot our possible witness, let's go see if we can help."

We go to Mr. Klink and he is not doing well. He is having difficult time breathing. I bend over close to him and ask, "Who else knew about the swamp?"

He can only whisper. I place my ear close to his mouth. He whispers a name. The EMTs arrive at the scene so Jim and I move away from the area.

Once we get a safe distance, Jim asks, "What did he say?"

I look at Jim and pause for a second before answering. "He said Seymour Groves."

I get on my cell phone and call Detective Concile. After several rings, and what seems like an eternity, she answers, "Detective Concile."

I start in on her. "Sam, its Mickke D. What the hell is going on? I thought you told me you had eyes on all of my suspects. I think Seymour Groves just shot and maybe killed a possible witness with information on the killings!"

She tries to calm me down. "Slow down, Mickke D. What are you talking about? What happened?"

"I'm at the Oyster Bay Golf Course and I was talking with the person who told Jon Barry about Billybob Swamp. Someone just shot him. He whispered to me the name Seymour Groves. I am beginning to think that the guy I saw and Seymour Groves are one in the same person."

Now she is starting to get upset. "I'll call you right back."

Sam gets on her phone and calls Officer Evans, the person assigned to keep an eye on Seymour Groves. "Officer Evans here."

She calmly asks, "Evans, where is Mr. Groves?"

Evans replies, "Well, he hasn't left the condo building so I guess he's still inside."

Sam immediately asks, "Has anyone left the building recently?"

"Yeah, a guy left about an hour and a half ago, but he did not fit the description of Mr. Groves."

Sam thinks for a minute. "Is there a back door?"

"No, all of the condos open onto an inside corridor and he's on the third floor. Only the first-floor condos have a back way out."

"What did the man look like?"

"He was probably six feet tall, bald head, and he was wearing a leather jacket."

"Damn. Okay here's what I want you to do. I'm sending backup and once they get there go in and see if Mr. Groves is there. If the other guy comes back, arrest him. However, be careful, he could be our killer. Call me right away once you get inside the condo."

"Don't I need a warrant for that?"

Sam answers sternly, "Screw the warrant, knock the door down if you have to, I'll take the heat if need be."

Sam calls Woolever and Stratton to go meet Officer Evans and then she calls Mickke D back. "Mickke D, you may be right. A guy left Mr. Groves' condo building and he fit the description of the guy you saw at La Belle Amie Vineyard. My people are going in to see if Groves is there. I'll let you know as soon as I hear back from them."

৯৫

Jim and I go back to the office and after about an hour, I call the hospital. I ask for Bonnie Somerset, since she should remember me from my previous stay there. She answers and after a short chat, she checks and tells me that Mr. Klink made it through surgery and it looks like he's going to make a complete recovery. I call Sam and give her the good news. She may have a witness who can tie Seymour Groves to Billybob Swamp.

I am just hanging up with Sam when I hear Jim yell at me. "Mickke D, come in here, you need to see this."

I go back to Jim's office and he is staring at a photo on his desk. "I contacted the Bureau to see if they had any photos of any of your suspects. Here's what they just sent me on Seymour Groves."

I stare at the photo in disbelief. It is a picture of the guy I saw at La Belle Amie Vineyard, except with short dark brown curly hair and not coal black long hair and black framed glasses. Now I am sure Seymour Groves and our killer are one in the same person. The only question that remains now is where is he?

Chapter 65: The Condo Search

As soon as Woolever and Stratten arrive at Mr. Groves' condo building, they along with Officer Evans, knock on Seymour's door. No one answers. Officer Evans looks at Woolever and he nods. Officer Evans kicks in the door. All three enter, guns drawn.

The condo is empty. They look into each room and closet. Nothing. Seems to be a normal furnished condo, nice but not top-shelf. They all put on gloves and start to look around. They find very little personal items. It looks as if Seymour led a rather frugal life. Finally, Stratton says, "Come in the bathroom, I think I just found Seymour Groves."

With guns leading the way, Woolever and Officer Evans rush into the bathroom where Stratton is holding a medium-sized metal box, which she found beneath some cleaning supplies under the sink. She shows them the box and pulls out a black toupee and black framed clear, non-prescription glasses. Looking at Officer Evans she says, "No wonder you didn't see him leave. Seymour Groves was still here in the bathroom, he never left."

Woolever calls Sam and updates her with what they didn't find and what they did find. She tells him to stay until the forensic squad gets there and in the meantime, search the parking lot for a two-door gray pick-up truck. Mickke D said he thought he saw one leave Oyster Bay when the shooting took place. She also tells them to canvass the neighbors and see if any of them know anything about Mr. Groves.

⌘⌘

Seymour Groves is sitting across the street from his condo, not visible from the parking lot. He sees three people, one uniformed policeman and two plain-clothes cops, enter his building and come out about forty minutes later. He figured the authorities were getting close to coming for him so he put what little personal things he needed in the back of his pick-up truck along with all of his weapons, ammo, and his Harley. He covered everything with a tie-down tarp.

His mind is moving quickly and in several directions. He needs a place to hang out for a couple of days until the heat cools down. He figures they will be looking for him and his truck. He is also thinking about paying Mickke D a visit. He should have killed him at the condo instead of shooting that other guy.

He can't believe he left Seymour's toupee and glasses in the bathroom. After leaving Colorado, Seymour purchased the toupee in St. Louis and he bought the clear, black-framed glasses at a drugstore in Atlanta, on his way across country to Myrtle Beach. He decides that realistically he will eventually be caught and he is already thinking about his defense. He grins and slowly leaves the area.

                        ৰ৶

Sam puts out a wanted bulletin for Seymour Groves along with a vague description of his pick-up truck. Woolever and Stratten talk with several of the neighbors and most of them say the same thing, "Mr. Groves was not very social and he pretty much kept to himself." They say they did see another man there occasionally and when Woolever shows them the sketch of Mickke D's suspect, they say, "yes, that is the guy." They say the man in the sketch used to ride a Harley but they never saw Mr. Groves on it. As a matter of fact, they say they never saw the two men together.

Sam can do nothing now except wait and see if someone turns up something or some civilian calls in a tip. She figures he will ditch the truck for another vehicle and leave the area, but she is not sure.

As the word spreads around town, she gets several calls from women who had dated Seymour and they seem very happy to be alive. The majority of them said they never had a second date with the man. He was strange once they were alone with him. Sam asked the women if he had hurt any of them but most of them said not to the extent of calling the police.

Chapter 66: A Peaceful Evening

It's Friday night and I am at ease in my La-Z-Boy. I'm reading the latest Steve Barry novel and there is a bottle of Heineken on the end table. I'm seriously thinking about getting out of the private investigator business. Maybe I will just stay active in real estate to give me something to do. Jim can run the PI business by himself. My eyes are starting to close and Blue, stretched out on my sheet-covered couch, is snoring.

Finally, a relaxing night at home. The serial killer has been identified, everyone in the world is looking for him, and no one has been killed lately. Cathy now knows what happened to her friend and I have stopped looking over my shoulder at everyone who has no hair and a leather jacket.

My Colombian problem went away and I hope it never returns. My only source of anxiety has to do with Beverly. I still can't believe she just left without saying goodbye or anything and I still can't believe Jim's theory that she is CIA. I guess I may have cared for her more than I wanted to admit, of course, not to the extent of becoming my fourth wife but maybe as a very special friend for a long time. It would be nice to run in to her again sometime. I have a lot of unanswered questions.

I start to nod off again. I guess it's time to take Blue out and go to bed. As I place my book on the end table, I notice Blue's ears perk up. He then sits up and I can hear a low growl coming from deep inside his body. The hair begins to stand up on his back. Something is wrong. The doorbell rings and we are both startled. Usually when the doorbell rings, Blue can't wait to get to the door with tail wagging to see who has come to visit him. This time he is not moving. His growl becomes a little louder and deeper.

I look at the atomic clock on the wall and it reads 10:50. I whisper to Blue to stay. For once, he obeys. The only person who would be at my door this time of night would be my neighbor Jim and he always calls ahead of time. Maybe it's Beverly, but Blue would know if it was her. The bell rings again. I reach for my .45, which is also on the end table, along with my beer. Just as I stand up and switch off the only light in the room, the first blast from a shotgun explodes through the right-hand window beside my door. I feel pain in my left arm and I end up on the couch next to Blue. The second blast takes out the left-hand window and the painted mirror on the far wall. The third blast blows a hole in my storm door and tears apart my metal front door. Someone on the other side of my front door does not like me.

My first inclination is to use the spray and pray method of returning fire, just unload my .45 on the front door and listen to hear if anyone falls or moans. However, I quickly dismiss that idea since there are two houses right across the street from my front door. The shooting ends and I hear a vehicle depart rather hurriedly.

The next thing I hear is Jim's voice. "Mickke D, its Jim, don't shoot. Are you okay?"

As soon as Blue hears Jim's voice, he runs to the front door and begins to whine. "Yeah Jim, I think so, come on in." I painfully reach up and switch my lamp back on.

"Which hole do you want me to come through?"

"I don't care, take your pick."

The light shows me the destruction to my front entrance. Jim, along with his .44 Super Blackhawk in hand, manages to make his way through the carnage and says, "My God, did you piss off one of your ex-wives again?"

"I don't think so, but I would venture to guess Seymour Groves has not left town yet."

The next thing I hear are sirens and then I see the reflection of blue lights and red lights coming down River Bluff Lane. A fire truck and an EMT vehicle pull up in front of my house, followed closely by two police cars. I recognize one of the police officers as

Officer Doan but the other one is new. I haven't seen him before. At least Detective Concile hasn't shown up to razz me.

An EMT comes in and looks at my arm. They tell me it looks as if a couple of the shotgun pellets went through the fleshy part of my arm, no big deal. They wrap a bandage around my arm and ask me if I want to go to the ER. I tell them no thanks and that I will see my doctor as soon as possible.

Officer Doan is next in line. He looks at Jim with his huge weapon in hand and then says to me, "Man, did you piss someone off lately?"

I do a double take and look at Jim who places his gun in the small of his back. "Why does everyone think I pissed someone off?"

"Well, this looks like it's very personal to me. The person who did this does not like you," Doan replies.

"Really, what was your first clue?"

I had no more than uttered the above when through the front door destruction comes Detective Concile. She is not dressed in her usual pants suit, but in blue jeans and a light jacket. As usual, she begins shaking her head the moment she sees me. "Mickke D, I think you need to get into a different line of work. Maybe you should stick to selling real estate and teaching golf."

"I'm fine thank you and I was just thinking the same thing earlier this evening. I would venture to say you have not captured Seymour Groves?"

She gets a funny look on her face. "No we haven't. Why, you think he did this?"

"I would be willing to bet a whole bunch of money he did this."

She changes the subject. "We found three 12-gauge shotgun shells outside. Must have been a pump. You're lucky he didn't come right in firing."

"I'm going to bet he didn't think he got me and I would be waiting for him. He would have been right."

Sam looks at Jim. "Mr. Bolin, isn't it? Did you see anything?

"Sorry detective, I was more concerned about getting over here but some type of a vehicle left just seconds before I came out of my door. I think it was a pick-up truck but there were no lights on it so I really couldn't tell."

By 12:30, everyone has left and the neighbors have all gone back inside, turned off their lights, and gone to bed once Sam had a patrol car stationed in the cul-de-sac. The firefighters helped Jim and I bring plywood from under the house, which I had made to cover my windows in case of a hurricane. They nailed it to my front entrance and I will use the back sliding door entrance until I get a handy man in to replace my doors and front windows. Jim says Blue and I can stay at his place tonight, but I decline.

Once in bed my demons begin to move around and I can't get to sleep. I thought my trip to Colombia had been my last hunting trip but it looks like I have to make one more trip back into my demon-filled world. However, this time I will be going alone and I will tell no one where and when I am going. I think I know where Seymour is hiding out.

Chapter 67: The End Is Near

Where is the one place where the police probably are not searching? I'm guessing Billybob Swamp. No one would think that Seymour, or whatever he calls himself, would go back to the scene of the crime, the place where he dumped the bodies. No one at the condo development actually saw him in the pick-up truck because he always parked away from his rented condo and walked to and from. Therefore, there is not a good description of the truck. I think he is moving around during the day in a disguise, possibility on his Harley and camping out in his truck at night at the swamp. I also believe he wants to kill me before he leaves the area. Therefore, instead of waiting for him to come after me, I am going after him.

While I was at the swamp with Sam, I paid very close attention to the area and when I got home, I went on Google Earth and looked at the area again. I noticed a clearing about 100 yards west of the location where they found the bodies. It is off the trail and not easy to spot. It looked to me like an excellent place for someone to setup camp.

≈∞≈

After I settled with my insurance company over the total loss of my Trailblazer, I added a few bucks and bought myself a new vehicle. I had never owned a brand new car and I had never owned a Cadillac. Therefore, I bought myself a Cadillac SRX. Since I liked to get down and dirty every once in a while and go places where I didn't want to take the Caddy, I also purchased a used Chevy Silverado, which Mark also uses, occasionally, for the landscape business. Tonight will be a truck night.

I wait until dark to load up the truck for my trek into the swamp. I put on my old jungle fatigues, boots, a floppy hat, and I put camouflage on my face. I take my .45 and an AR-15 with a night scope. Colonel T gave me the AR-15 and scope after I gave him the list of welcome visitors I picked up at Valdez's compound. I also have extra ammo for each. As I am ready to leave, I feel the demons deep in my gut start to move around.

The closer I get to the swamp, the more my demons begin to roar. I remember Colonel T telling me that fear acted as a stimulant, sharpening the mind's ability to think. I am now focusing all of my senses on eliminating Seymour as a threat and nothing else. If Seymour is where I think he is, only one of us will come out of the swamp alive.

ॐ∽

Seymour is exactly where Mickke D thinks he is, but he has no idea that he, like the cougar in Colorado, will soon become the hunted. He figures to stay in the area for a few more days and take one more shot at Mickke D. He also figures by waiting a little while longer, the police will slow down their surveillance of local roads and highways. He has an appointment just outside of Loris tomorrow to have his light gray truck painted a candy apple red by some less than upstanding local citizens. Once the truck is painted, he will feel better about getting on the road after one last-ditch effort to eliminate Mickke D.

ॐ∽

Before I get to the turnoff into the swamp, I switch off my lights. A half moon fills the night with a pale glow, so driving the short distance is not a real problem. The road into the swamp becomes not much more than a trail about a hundred yards in. I park the truck at the point where the two-lane road turns into a one-lane trail, only wide enough for one vehicle and there is swamp on either side. I don't want anyone getting in or out driving a vehicle. I exit the truck and quietly close the door. I gather up my rifle, put on dark-colored gloves, which, along with the long sleeves on my shirt and the mosquito repellent in the camouflage on my face and neck, with any luck, will ward off the bugs. I take a deep breath and start down the trail, which is moist, so a slow walk is noiseless. I notice tire tracks on the trail and they look as if they were made recently. I stop as the sounds from the creatures in the swamp go from a soft hum to complete silence. It's as if they know there is a predator in their domain. Within seconds, the soft hum begins again. I move on.

Being alone in a swamp at night can be a very scary thing. However, I learned a long time ago that it is mind over matter. You need a mindset that you're the predator and the swamp creatures are more afraid of you than you are of them. I just hope the alligators realize this.

I stop as I near the point where the rescue squad found the bodies. I crouch down, raise my rifle, and survey the area through my night scope. I am able to observe a pick-up truck parked just off the side of the trail leading down to the lake. It looks like the same one I saw leaving Oyster Bay. I see no movement. He may have parked the truck here so that anyone coming in would think someone is night fishing. I shoulder my rifle, pull out my .45, and venture slowly toward the truck. I circle the truck quietly and gaze in the windows. The truck is empty. I touch the hood and it is still warm. He must have just recently returned. I lift up the tarp covering the bed of the truck and I see a Harley. I now know for sure that Seymour is here somewhere.

I walk slowly and carefully back to the main trail. With each step I take, I seem to slip farther and farther back into the black world of demons and death. However, I don't seem to mind because only in that environment will I survive. As I turn to my right and proceed toward the clearing, I get a whiff of citronella, which when burned is a way of fending off mosquitoes. I am getting close. Within a few minutes, I see a faint light, probably from a lantern. Ripples of concern are beginning to ebb through me. Am I up for this? The demons are swirling around in my mind with so many conflicting thoughts it is hard for me to concentrate. I make a mistake and step on a dry branch. The crack of the branch emits a deafening roar.

The next thing I hear is silence. The creatures are mute and the light has disappeared. So much for the element of surprise. I decide to move slowly away from the broken branch in case he figures out where the sound came from. Just as I move, two shots ring out and the area where the branch was located is pelted with buckshot. I feel pain in my left arm. I look at my shirtsleeve and I can see a dark stain. It's blood. That's the same arm he shot me in before. I grab a handkerchief from my pocket and with the help of my teeth, I tie it around my arm.

Since moving slowly didn't work, this time I take off running while watching for a muzzle flash before I return fire. So far, I don't believe he knows if I am really out here. I would like to keep it that way for a while.

The tree seemed to materialize out of nowhere. I hit it hard, knocking the wind out of my lungs. Pain blossoms in my arm and shoulder, but I manage to stay on my feet. As I lean against the tree and try to catch my breath, I'm beginning to wonder if this was a good idea.

From beside the tree, and after I am able to breathe freely again, I slowly turn and aim my rifle in the vicinity where I remember seeing the light. Nothing is moving but I can hear erratic footsteps of someone moving quickly from one place to another, as if stopping to hide or listen.

The next sound I hear is a man's voice. "That you, Mickke D? I didn't think you would find me out here. I guess I underestimated your ability."

I still don't think he knows for sure I'm here so I opt not to answer but I do aim my rifle in the direction of his voice. He has to be feeling intimidated. If I am here, he has no way out but to go through me or go deeper into the swamp. Not knowing has to be driving him crazy. Again he calls out, "Did I hit you, Mickke D? You do know they all deserved what they got, don't you?"

Still, I don't answer. I look through the scope once more and he is half standing up. He is getting brave. I can make out what looks like a shotgun in his hand. I judge the distance from me to him at no more than fifty yards away. Should I twist the knife a little bit or just shoot his sorry ass?

From behind the tree, I twist the knife. "Sorry Seymour, you missed. Better luck next time."

"I'm not Seymour. Seymour is a wimp compared to me." Two more shots ring out but both fall harmlessly in the direction of the broken branch on the trail. He has no idea where I am.

"You know Mickke D, no jury will find me guilty. I'm crazy. Maybe I'll just give up and you can take me in. What do you think?"

After a pause, I answer him back. "If you're not Seymour, then who are you?"

"I'm his alter ego. I do the things he won't do." Two more shots are fired and again they are nowhere close to me.

"Is that your way of giving up?" I call out.

He fails to answer but I do hear footsteps moving around again. "So what should I call you?"

"How about Jimmie or Leroy. It doesn't really make any difference. Just not Seymour. I really don't care for him."

He is right, he will probably not be convicted by a jury. And he's also right about being crazy. What type of person in their right mind would ever do what he did to those victims?

I twist the knife again. "So Seymour, are you going to give up and come out?"

"Damnit, I told you not to refer to me as Seymour. Are you deaf or just plain stupid?" he rants.

I can tell he is really irritated now. "So, whoever you are, drop the shotgun, raise your hands, and step out into the clearing."

I watch through my scope as he drops the shotgun but he reaches behind his back and pulls out a handgun. "Okay Mickke

D, I dropped the shotgun and I'm moving to the clearing. Don't shoot."

I've spent enough time with this lowlife killer. I put my scope back on him and pull the trigger. The soft whine of a sound suppressor waffles through the swamp and Seymour goes down.

He cries out, "You bastard, you shot me!"

I was aiming at his head. I guess I hit him in the arm or shoulder. "Sorry Seymour, I was aiming at your head. Now, throw out the handgun and we'll get this over with."

The bully is no longer in control. "What handgun? Help me, I'm going to bleed to death."

My demons are now speaking for me. "Get your ass out on that trail or I'm going to throw a grenade and blow your sorry ass away."

My inner demons are forcing me into a place ruled only by revenge. I have always considered myself as a tough, gusty, decisive type of guy, one who accepts the situation thrust upon me, doing what needs to be done. My mind hovers for several minutes in an endless abyss. I try to fight off the tsunami of black thoughts that are invading my mind. Then, I remembered something someone once told me. I whisper, "Good people sometimes do bad things, but they may need to be done."

Seymour moves from his cover out into the open clearing and onto the trail. He walks toward me with one arm in the air and the other at his side. I watch him through my scope until he gets about twenty yards away. I dash out of my hiding place, my .45 in hand and before he can utter a word or raise his lowered arm, I shoot him in the leg. He crumbles to the ground. I rush up to him and grab him by his wounded arm. He cries out in pain. I yell at him, "How does that feel, Seymour? Is that how your victims felt when you shot or stabbed them?"

He doesn't answer me. He just grins. I kick his gun away, jerk him to his feet, and push him back to where his truck is located. I throw him to the ground, get the truck keys from his pocket, and start the truck. I back it out and then point it toward the lake. I put the gearshift in neutral and pull on the parking brake. Next, I grab him and push him into the driver's seat. I grab a vine from a nearby tree and tie his hands to the steering wheel.

"Why did you kill those people, Seymour? What could they have possibly done to you for you to murder them like that?"

"They rejected me, you bastard! They didn't like me. And what's it to you?"

"*You* are the bastard, Seymour, one sick bastard."

Finally, he realizes his fate. "What are you going to do? You can't do this. I want a jury trial. I turned myself in to you. I need a doctor."

I then look him straight in the eyes and say, "Were your victims alive or dead when you sent them to a watery grave? If they were alive, you're going to experience the agonizing pain they felt when their lungs were craving for air but could breathe only water."

All of a sudden, I pause and look around. I am searching for those children who were peering out of the window at Valdez's home. They are nowhere to be seen. It's just him and me. I pull the parking brake off, put it in gear, and close the door. The truck slowly drives into the lake. Seymour cries out in fear. Before long, he will try to scream as electrifying pain soars though his lungs and finds his brain. I watch as the truck slowly sinks into the lake and the bubbles finally disappear.

I police the area. I pick up everything from his camp along with his shotgun and handgun and throw everything into the swamp. I turn away from the lake and slowly walk back to my truck. Taking a life is never easy. The act comes with consequences, the fear of which can absolutely paralyze a person, especially when they have a choice of whether to allow that person to live or die. And yet, I believe all of us have some of the killer mentality in us, but when the majority of us get to the point of pulling the trigger, we are able to take a step back. People like Seymour who have killed and killed again never even blink. They have been living in that abyss for years.

The closer I get to home, the quieter my demons become. As I pull into the driveway, I am almost completely calm and at ease. I had a job to do and I did it. It won't be easy but I will put this night out of my mind and go on with my life. Even though what I did was wrong, it needed to be done. Seymour's victims have been avenged.

Chapter 68: Case Closed

Six weeks later, I get a call from Detective Concile. "Mickke D, thought I would let you know we finally found Seymour Groves."

I pause as my pulse quickens. "Great, did you find him out west somewhere?"

"No, some fisherman found him floating in Billybob Swamp. It looks like he was shot and then dumped in the swamp. Divers also found his pick-up truck and a Harley in the swamp. You wouldn't know anything about that, would you?"

Again, I pause before answering. "No, detective, I would not, but I do have an observation."

She sighs. "And pray tell what might that be?"

"Sounds as if he picked on someone who fought back and you know what? Society has been served and the beach is now a safer place."

"Is that a confession, Mickke D?"

"No detective, just an observation."

࿔∽࿕

Sam looks at the file folder on her desk as well as the plastic baggie with two bullets taken from the body of Seymour Groves. A .223 from an AR-15 and a .45, Mickke D's weapon of choice The name on the folder is Seymour Groves. She writes a note with her black Sharpie, which reads "not enough evidence to pursue." She smiles and says to herself, "Thanks Mickke D." She stamps the file "Case Closed."

Final Chapter

From what I've been able to learn, Stephanie, Karen, Jenny, and Pat, are still at large, although I think half of the police in the world are looking for them. Most people feel they are on an island in the South Pacific enjoying the good life. The artifacts stolen from TC's warehouse also have not surfaced; however, Governor Craig has been easy on us since I reminded her that she was actually the one who agreed to hire the girls to help TC.

We have hired a new crew to help with the salvage work, two very competent guys and one stunningly lovely girl named Glenda. I may start spending more quality time at the salvage site. TC and I go out about once every two weeks to see if we can discover where Captain Swinely buried his treasure but so far, we have come up empty. We can't agree where to search. He keeps taking us around Hobcaw Barony and I like to search around Murrells Inlet. I suppose neither one of us are right. The treasure is probably right in front of our eyes. We just can't see it.

Since I'm already in the Pawleys Island vicinity, I usually call Bess's girlfriend Susan, and we have dinner and usually dessert at her house. Nothing serious, just friends with benefits.

TC has invited me to take some time off and go for a cruise with him to the Caribbean. He has a lead on another possible salvage job. I suppose I'll go along. I need a vacation. I have been having a strange nightmare lately; I see Seymour's pick-up truck and Valdez is kneeling in the bed of the truck. He has a bag of cocaine tied around his neck and his mouth is taped shut. Behind him, standing, are the two kids from Colombia I saw in the window and they have blindfolds covering their eyes. Seymour is looking out the back window and laughing. As the pick-up hits the water, it explodes and I wake up in a cold sweat. Yes, I need a vacation and I doubt if I can get into any trouble in the Caribbean. But then again, I've said that before. I think trouble sometimes follows me around.

❧❧

Beverly Beery walks into a McDonald's not far from Stone Mountain, Georgia. As soon as she walks through the door, she has a hot flash scamper through her loins. The restaurant reminds her of Mickke D. The steamy thought quickly passes. She orders a coffee and takes a seat in a booth on the far wall of the restaurant next to an exit. She looks over everyone in the restaurant and decides it is safe. She places a text on her cell phone to inform the person on the other end the coast is clear.

Five minutes later, Liz Woodkark enters the restaurant, orders a cup of coffee and takes a seat across from her. They exchange pleasantries and then Liz says, "So, do you think we will ever have a chance of recruiting that ex-boyfriend of yours Mickke D?"

Another hot flash dashes quickly through her body as she hears his name. "I don't think so, Liz. He doesn't need the money, he doesn't like taking orders and he is a loner, to say the least."

"Well, too bad. I think he would make a great agent."

"So Liz, is that why you wanted to meet with me today?"

"No Beverly, I have a job for you. I need a person found and I think you may know her."

Beverly asks with a quizzical look on her face, "And who might that be?"

Liz hands her a file folder. "Read this and then destroy it. Her name is Stephanie Langchester and she's a former British Intelligence agent."

"Sure, I met Stephanie once at a dinner party. She was there with three other girls. They were helping Mickke D's friend TC with some salvage work in Myrtle Beach."

Liz continues, "Well, it seems as if Stephanie and the girls split up after stealing Judge Cadium's boat and whatever they had found in the sunken pirate ship off the coast. It was not a happy break-up. Stephanie took off with all the money and left the girls high and dry. Now it seems as if the three girls have all been killed and British Intelligence thinks they have an ex-agent who has gone rogue."

Beverly looks strangely at Liz and asks, "So why doesn't British Intelligence take care of her and are they sure she killed the girls?"

"The Brits have been unable to find her and they would rather pay us to do the job. I'm looking into the murders now. I'll let you know what I find out, so be sure to contact me when you find her and I'll let you know whether to proceed or not. You'll receive a nice bonus check for this one. But be real careful, Stephanie is good."

Beverly smiles and replies, "No problem, so am I." She is curious. "So where am I going to look for her?"

"I've narrowed the search area down to the Caribbean. Do you think you can handle that?"

"Sure, sounds like a walk in the park or maybe a walk on the beach. I can use a paid vacation. Thanks Liz, I'll call you when I find her."

Liz stands up. "And Beverly, try not to get romantically involved with anyone this time."

"No problem Liz, I learned my lesson."

Liz leaves first. Beverly follows about ten minutes later. Another hot flash scurries through her body as she leaves the restaurant.

Excerpt from Steve's first book *Murder on the Front Nine.*

I am on my way to the police station and after giving my statement today, I am going to go down to Murrells Inlet and pick up the belongings of Rusty McRichards and ship them off to Barry. I have a funny feeling Rusty is also a part of the puzzle.

I am not concerned about giving my statement to Sam. After all, I took hundreds of statements myself while working for Army JAG at Fort Bragg.

Sam takes me into her office, which is rather small, poorly lit, and very cold. It's then that I get my first up-close and personal look at Detective Sam Concile. She is a very attractive woman probably about my age, mid-forties. She has bleached blond hair. Even in the dimly lit room, I can see the dark roots and she is dressed more like a real estate broker than a police detective might be. However, as we all know, looks can be deceiving.

"Please be seated Mr. MacCandlish."

She doesn't beat around the bush. She pulls out a folder, lays it on the desk and launches her attack, "Mickke MacCandlish, aka Mickke D, former Army Special Forces and investigative officer for Army JAG at Fort Bragg. I haven't found any record, not even a speeding ticket since you've been in the Myrtle Beach area. Real estate broker, landscape architect, golf teaching pro. Seems like the all-American boy. Anything else I should know about you, Mr. MacCandlish?"

I can't believe she has all of that information and nothing about the helicopter landing in the fairway behind my house or the altercation at Crab Catchers.

I answer, "Not that I can think of, that about covers it, except you didn't mention my three ex-wives, maybe they are still not happy with me."

See Steve's website www.stevenmcmillen.com.